TOM CLANCY'S NET FORCE

*Don't miss any of these exciting adventures
starring the teens of the Net Force . . .*

VIRTUAL VANDALS

The Net Force Explorers go head-to-head with a group of teen-age pranksters on-line—and find out firsthand that virtual bullets can kill you!

THE DEADLIEST GAME

The virtual Dominion of Sarxos is the most popular wargame on the Net. But someone is taking the game *very* seriously . . .

TOM CLANCY'S
NET FORCE™

ONE IS THE LONELIEST NUMBER

CREATED BY

Tom Clancy and **Steve Pieczenik**

BERKLEY JAM BOOKS, NEW YORK

TOM CLANCY'S NET FORCE: ONE IS THE LONELIEST NUMBER

A Berkley Jam Book / published by arrangement with
Netco Partners

PRINTING HISTORY
Berkley Jam edition / April 1999

The Penguin Putnam Inc. World Wide Web site address is
http://www.penguinputnam.com

ISBN: 0-425-16417-9

BERKLEY JAM BOOKS®
Berkley Jam Books are published by The Berkley Publishing Group,
a member of Penguin Putnam Inc.,
375 Hudson Street, New York, New York 10014.
BERKLEY JAM and its logo are trademarks
belonging to Berkley Publishing Corporation.

PRINTED IN THE UNITED STATES OF AMERICA

10 9 8 7 6 5 4 3 2 1

We'd like to thank the following people, without whom this book would have not been possible: Diane Duane, for help in rounding out the manuscript; Martin H. Greenberg, Larry Segriff, Denise Little, and John Helfers at Tekno Books; Mitchell Rubenstein and Laurie Silvers at BIG Entertainment; Tom Colgan of Penguin Putnam Inc.; Robert Youdelman, Esquire; and Tom Mallon, Esquire; and Robert Gottlieb of the William Morris Agency, agent and friend. We much appreciated the help.

I

It was five-thirty A.M. and still dark on the tarmac at Muroc. In a sky beginning to shade from black to indigo, the brightest stars still shone with that particular hasty flicker that betrays very cold air above. When you stepped on them, the weeds at the edge of the tarmac crunched, just faintly, with a thin bloom of high-desert frost. Away beyond the runway, somewhere out in the shadowy half-seen wilderness of Joshua trees and scrub and tumbleweed, a mockingbird involved in an intense territorial dispute with another of his kind was singing, one after another, the songs of every bird he knew—an impossible collection, winter songs and summer ones together, along with catcalls and wolf whistles and the occasional bad imitation of someone starting up a jet engine. Madeline Green, or Maj as she was called by her numerous friends, stood there in the dark. She smiled briefly at the mostly melodious racket the bird was making at this godawful hour, and then turned toward the reason she had come.

It stood silhouetted against the brightening crimson line of dawn, a shadow that could as yet cast no shadow of its own. At 189 feet long, thirty feet high, and 105 feet from wing tip to wing tip, the long sleek shape stood there dead quiet in the predawn glow, beginning, as she walked closer to it, to look silvery-ashen in the light of the late full moon just setting in the farthest west. Maj's sneakers made only the slightest sound on the tarmac as she approached. This was just as it should have been, since the ground crew had covered this stretch of ground first thing yesterday, removing every pebble and speck of gravel, or anything else, on the long "grooming" walk that finally saw them, at day's end, some fourteen thousand feet down the runway laid out on the dry salt lake bed. They would drive it and "fine groom" it again once this morning, just to be sure. No one wanted anything small and preventable to go wrong in a program in which so much had gone wrong already. . . .

Maj stopped by the huge right wing tip and looked up at it. It hung out over her like the roof of an oversized carport, some twenty feet above her head, a hint of the rose and gold of the morning at the edge of the world now beginning to sheen underneath it and show her faint shadows of the delicate brazing lines that had made its construction possible. Buried inside that wing was a vertical honeycomb of steel so thin that it could easily be mistaken for foil; a whole battery of new techniques had had to be devised to "weld" the steel together into a structure strong enough to be a wing, but light enough (despite the wing's huge size) to let the plane lift off the ground.

When it did, the plane would ride her own compression wave; the shock wave generated by the passage through the air of that long, pointed nose would be trapped under the broad triangular wing behind, producing more lift than any other flight configuration known. For all her half-million pounds' weight, she flew light . . . and fast. She would cruise at Mach 2 and "dash" to Mach 3, or better . . . no one was sure how much better. No one had yet pushed her to the outside of her huge envelope.

Except Maj . . . and she was going to do it again today. She hoped. . . .

In the early morning cold, she shivered. And laughed again, for the cold was virtual, as virtual as the sky, or the ship herself. Maj was simming.

She walked under the huge body of the plane, went slowly over to the landing gear, and rested her hand on one of the three-foot-high tires on the starboard bogie. The tire was not real, but *it* thought it was. Maj had spent nearly a day writing just the portion of code that ran the physical characteristics of the tires in this simulation. If she got into the plane and put it through a duplicate of its very first flight, the brakes would dutifully fail on landing, and the wheel would lock up, and when it did, the tire would catch fire just as enthusiastically as the original had, on that long-ago sunny morning in 1964.

The whole plane, in fact, would act exactly as it had on its initial flight . . . though she would try to stop it from doing so in *all* regards. That was the challenge of this particular simulation. She had been working on it, on and off, for nearly a year now. Naturally she hadn't written every line of the code herself—the simulation composition software was there to help her with the repetitive parts of the work—but it was all Maj's brainchild. She had researched every aspect of the materials used to build the plane, the motivations of the people who had designed it (as far as they could be worked out at this distance in time), the engineering quirks, the hiccups in the weather during testing . . . everything. Maj figured that she now knew this plane better than the people who had designed it. This was hard to be *completely* sure about—the people in question were almost all dead. But she thought they would have been pleased with her anyway. Through her efforts, the North American XB-70 Valkyrie supersonic bomber lived again . . . and flew.

''*Ho-yo-to-ho*, babydoll,'' Maj said softly under her breath; it was Wagner's transcription, in his operas, of the Valkyries' battle cry. She scraped absently at the rubber of the massive tire with one fingernail, looking toward the brightening east. Away out in the desert, the mockingbird sang on in harmonies that had more to do with Schoenberg than Wagner, and some other, smaller bird started an unconscious and insolent counterpoint.

The others would be coming along soon. Maj was not at all alone in her love of simming—the art of building, and using, the perfect virtual simulation of an object or event inside one's own ''playroom,'' a personal space like the old-fashioned ''web pages,'' though much more fully interactive than even the best of those static pages had ever been. Maj was a little more mechanically minded about simming, maybe, than some of the informal group she worked with. Some of them were more interested in simming in the historical mode.

Bob, for example, had been working on a reproduction of

the Battle of Gettysburg for nearly two years now. Maj had spent more time than she cared to consider in places that stank abominably of black powder, where she couldn't see a thing farther than a foot away from her because of the smoke of cannon fire, and where she kept jumping when the archaic shrapnel of "canister" went through her—without doing her any harm, of course. The shrapnel was deadly only to the equally virtual soldiers in the reproduction.

That was another problem with Bob's simulation, from Maj's point of view. He was a stickler for getting the gore right, and after yet another run-through of one or another portion of his version of Gettysburg, Maj would come back into the real world and find she had no appetite for dinner. The others teased him, telling him he should be as fanatical about the characters' uniforms as he was about the shape and color of their fallen-out insides. Bob would respond that he was getting the important stuff right first. Some of the others thought that explanation sort of made sense, but mostly it made Maj wonder about the state of some of Bob's interior organs, specifically his brains.

Other simulations were more benign, at least from her point of view. Fergal was into "classic"-period wheeled automobiles, from the beginning of the last century to about the mid-1930's, and kept reproducing cars that ran on steam or had strange names like Humber.

Sander had the hots for the peculiar and hybrid aircraft that had been somewhat frantically designed by Germany toward the end of World War II, the so-called "Secret Project" planes—a bizarre assortment of fledgling flying saucers and VTOL (or vertical-takeoff-and-landing) tail-sitters powered by ramjets mounted at the ends of helicopter rotors, and heaven only knows what else. It was one of these that had been the last sim that the whole group had attended, a week ago, and Maj had to admit she'd laughed as hard as the rest when the *Triebflügel*'s simulation program had failed and the engines had flown off the ends of the rotors, destroying half the buildings that Sander had scattered around his virtual airfield and killing most of his virtual ground crew.

Kelly was fascinated by submarines, and was reconstructing one by one the weird steam-powered subs with which the British fleet had been experimenting around the end of the First World War, the ''K boats''—submarines so hurried in their building and so flawed in their design that Maj couldn't understand how Kelly got them to function. But function they did, provoking even the least interested of the simming group to admit that they were impressed by what Kelly had done.

It wasn't just the simulation that was designed to impress, of course. No sim was complete unless it was set against the proper background. The goal was to mock-up a given moment in time as completely and accurately as possible—''recreation'' in the purest sense of the word. Little things counted. Maj looked over at the massive main strut of the landing gear she stood by, and ran a finger slowly down the cold metal. The thinnest bloom of frost came away where she touched. She lifted her finger to squint at it very closely, and watched the individual crystals of frost melt. She had programmed every one of them. Well, not individually. Some of this was ''fractal'' programming, in which you introduced a set of patterns for a given physical behavior and instructed the program to apply that set of rules across the environment, though uniquely in each new occurrence, or (since you could too heavily burden the computer's processing power that way) at least on the close order of ''uniquely.'' Maj was glad that the records confirmed the temperature had dropped below freezing on this particular night. Frost was easier to code than rain, and prettier.

Maj paused for a moment and glanced idly up . . . then suddenly realized that she was looking at a spot on the belly of the plane, to the left of the bomb-bay doors, where the paint was peeling again. This was not a genuine problem, at least as far as the simulation went. It *had* been a problem for the original XB-70 early in its career, and the cause for a lot of confusion until the techs had worked out the source of the problem. The guys at the hangar had kept giving the Valkyrie fresh coats of paint each time she went up for one or another of the Air Force VIPs, and as a result the flexion of her skin caused by the high temperatures during flight had made her crack the paint and ''shed'' it raggedly away. But Maj could have sworn she'd instructed the master simulation manager to do away with the peeling for this run. For one thing, the techs had eventually realized that one thin coat of white anti-flash paint was all she needed, so this was a "legal" intervention on her part. For another, there were some of Maj's group who would see the peeling paint and start making fun of it, refusing despite the evidence to believe that it was a genuine "design feature" and not a bug.

Maj breathed out. *Roddy* . . .

"Code," Maj said to the simulation.

"Authorization," said the composition software.

"Five eighteen fifty-two," she said. It was her grand-mother's birthday.

"Authorized. Action?"

"Show me the paint subroutines," Maj said.

The space around her briefly subdivided itself, so that she was looking both at the Valkyrie and at line after line of bright text hovering in the air. Not all the code was in text form. Some of it was object-oriented. A group of six paint "chips" about a foot square appeared in the air before her. Each of them was tagged with a small glowing spot, the hyperlink to its other physical characteristics.

"Selection routine," Maj said.

"Listening."

"Set paint chip selection zero three."

"Done."

"Remove all paint on object."

"Done," said the composition software, and as it did, the plane flushed the palest possible silver-rose, dawn on bare metal.

"Apply one coat of zero three."

"Done." And the plane was white again, still catching that pale sheen from the setting moon on this side, reflecting the eastern light pinkly on her belly and her roof and her high "twin" tail.

"Store paint subroutines; save this change to the proto-type," Maj said to the computer.

"Done."

"Finished. Save out."

"Saved," said the computer, and fell silent.

Maj sighed and looked up at the Valkyrie again, then slowly started her walk-round, looking to see that she hadn't forgotten anything as obvious as the paint. *Are both the wings here? Yup. Both the tails? Yup. Anything leaking that shouldn't be leaking? Nope. Any cracks? Any holes besides the ones the designers put in?*

It was something more than the usual walk-round that a pilot might have done, for Maj was also checking for differences in the plane that had no right to be there: details from later versions or different versions of the model. On some long-lived aircraft, like the Spitfire or its rival, the Messerschmitt Bf 109, you could get into a bewildering number of variants, and heaven help you if one of your eagle-eyed simming buddies caught something in your plane that shouldn't have been there. Your only hope was that they hadn't read your code completely enough, or your background material . . . or that they hadn't done further research of their own on your project. Knowing this bunch, though, some of whom appeared to have no lives beyond simming, Maj figured this was a pretty faint hope.

The rules under which they operated this "game" were tough, and meant to be so. The Group of Seven—even though there were nine of them now, the name had stuck—had originally gathered together from various parts of the worldwide virtual Net to help each other with the stickier parts of simming by being what a simmer most needed: ruthless but friendly analysts of what was being simulated, and of the art of simming itself. You submitted the parameters of your present playroom to the group on a regular basis, and again whenever there were major changes: a shift in the version of your software, a change of computer platform, or of your implant or other means of access to the virtual world. When you were ready to have the others look at the simulation you were building in that playroom, you submitted your code to the group, or at least the relevant parts of the code, about ten days before a scheduled meet.

Then, when they'd all read it, everyone got together and watched you run your simulation. Afterwards, there was a bull session where they "graded" you—not quite the formal holding-numbers-up of a sports competition, but effective enough, and sometimes fairly scathing. It was taken with good enough grace by the members of the group, by and large, since the purpose really was to help each other get better at this business.

Some of the Group of Seven thought that simulation was something they wanted to do professionally when they were old enough to get into the job market. Some of them were intent on getting at the job market whether they were old enough or not—the simulations business could admittedly use all the talent it could find. There were some fourteen- and fifteen-year-old millionaires out there who had come up with one innovation or another that the market had to have at any price.

A couple of the group members, Fergal and Sander, Maj thought were particularly likely to succeed in this way. Fergal was so driven that the others were sure she had no life outside simming, and Sander, though almost exactly the opposite type from Fergal—he gave the impression that he thought it was all a big game—was nonetheless one of those brilliant types who suddenly, out of nowhere, stumbles across the Big Idea, possibly because he's already so completely prepared for it.

Maj doubted that she could ever go this route. She had too many other things she was interested in as well as simming, particularly her music and her own growing interest in systems design. But it was, as her mom would say, "one more string to her bow," and there was no harm in getting good at something which, if she persevered, could at least supply her with a job on the way to something else more interesting.

Maj rested her hand on the metalwork again. It was flushing more rose-colored in the growing dawn. "Okay, *Rosweisse*," she said under her breath, "let's go do the deed. . . ."

She went around the far side of the plane.

"Ladder," she said, and it appeared. Slowly and carefully, because the frost could make you slip, Maj climbed up the ladder to the cockpit.

"Canopy," she said. Obediently it lifted up and away in front of her.

There was already someone sitting in the right-hand seat. Brown hair, brown eyes, not too tall—which had always been a relief to Maj, at least since her older brother had started his growth spurt and begun banging his head into the tops of doorways—fairly slender, not a raving beauty but not bad-looking either, with eyes set wide so that she wore a sort of permanently surprised look. It was interesting the way your looks didn't really make an impression on you when you saw them every morning in the mirror—but this way, they did.

"Morning," she said.

"Theoretically," said Maj Two.

Maj had given a lot of thought to who would make a good copilot. She could have constructed one of the original pilots to help, but she was afraid her simulation might turn out too well, and start to make the same mistakes as the original. However, *if you want a job done right,* Maj's father seemed to say about every five seconds, *do it yourself,* and finally she had decided that that was just what she would do. Her copilot was a virtual copy of herself, carefully programmed with everything she and the XB-70's designers knew about the plane— but with her own preferences most carefully emphasized.

"How far along are you?" she said to her double.

"Not too far," said Maj Two, and grinned slightly. "I know I like to look over my shoulder. . . ."

Maj laughed briefly, wondering if she had perhaps spent more time or care on this part of the simulation than she realized. *Perfectionist,* she thought, but that was her dad's side of the family heredity coming out. He had no patience with sloppy work, or work half done . . . and in this particular case, neither had she.

Maj sat down in the left-hand seat and glanced across the instrument panel. It was less involved than the new Boeing-MDD 787, but not by much—a daunting array, until you got used to it. In the middle, above the throttles for the six J93 engines, were eighteen dials for air speed, hydraulic pressure, and various other more mundane functions. A set of indicators and dials and toggles above and below handled crew-alert systems, wing-tip-fold and landing-gear status, fire systems, and so forth. This was, of course, well before computers. All such matters were dealt with manually by the flight crew. The thought boggled Maj sometimes, considering that the pilots were also *testing* this aircraft, and theoretically had a lot of more important things to think about, such as what Mach she was doing, and whether she was staying airborne. Then, on either side, came the instruments for altitude, the Mach repeaters, test-recording equipment, and so on.

The instruments were all analog—some of them, like the controls for the radio frequency near the left top of the instrument panel, were actually little rotating drums that clicked along, one face at a time, as the numbers they were indicating changed. It all seemed astonishingly primitive. At the same time, this plane had some advantages. Being pretty much pre-transistor, it was nearly invulnerable to problems like the electromagnetic pulse that would accompany an atomic explosion.

She would have carried nukes eventually, Maj thought, easing herself into the left-hand seat. *Just as soon as she went into service . . .* That was one of the only things that slightly tarnished the simulation for her. In this incarnation, the plane was merely a testbed for high-Mach technology. But her range and speed had very early suggested to the Air Force bigwigs that she should be delivering nukes. Only the shooting down of Francis Gary Powers's U-2 in 1961, with its lesson that the surface-to-air missiles were improving a lot faster than planes were, had diverted the Valkyries from that mission. It had caused their program to be canceled too, as well as that of the F-108 Rapier, which would have been the Valkyrie's fighter escort.

Maj's feelings about this twist of fate were profoundly mixed. This beautiful aircraft had produced no Hiroshimas or Nagasakis . . . and had she been available for use in 1963, when the Cuban missile crisis had heated up to almost boiling over, there was no telling what might have happened, especially with General Curtis LeMay repeatedly urging the President to strike the first blow.

But at the same time, Maj dearly wished that the Valkyrie could have gone on to be built as she should have been, a peerless bomber, a weapon ready to be used if there had really been need to use her. No one else on Earth would have had anything that could cope with her . . . though how long the advantage would have lasted, there was no telling. Military superiority was, of all kinds of superiority, the most fleeting, she knew, especially when all sides playing the deadly game were really serious.

Maj sat back and sighed. She put her feet on the rudder

pedals and jiggled them a little. They resisted—the hydraulics were still down, as they would be until well along in the engine-start sequence.

"You're really not very far along," she said to her twin.

"Neither were they at this point," said Maj Two. "Come on, let's do it."

"Right." Maj reached down to the paperwork-clip mounted on the left side of the gray brushed-metal throttle pedestal, and came up with the well-thumbed checklist, tossing its grimy cover back over the ring-binding at the top and starting the first page. "Radio call . . ."

"Niner-six point zero zero one," said her counterpart, leaning over to check it against the list on the copilot's seat.

"Crew warning lights . . ."

"Encapsulate OK; bailout OK."

"EWS/ENS brake?"

"One, two, three on and OK."

"EWS/ADS agent discharge . . ."

"Both up."

"EWER engine brake . . ."

"One, two, three, all off."

"Time," Maj said.

"Five thirty-three, September twenty-one, nineteen sixty-four."

"Not that time, you spud. Time outside."

"Twenty zero three, October twenty, twenty twenty-five."

"Thank you. Shock pos—"

"Bypass area one go, two go."

"Meatball—"

Abruptly her father's face appeared in the space where the cockpit's front canopy would have been if it were down, and Maj started at the sight of him. She had installed a link to "outside" audio and video as a heads-up display, but right now there was nothing *but* her dad's head, apparently hanging in midair, and the effect was peculiar, especially where the "matte" effect caused by the computer's processing of the image sparkled a little in the places where his hair was starting to go missing.

"Hi, Dad," she said. "Blinding . . ."

"What is?"

"Your head—you're standing right under that lamp again. Can you move a little to one side?"

He did, making an amused face, and the lighting on his head changed somewhat, though his face remained centered. "I just wanted to make sure you'd finished your homework."

She snorted. "Oh, please!"

"And what about you?" her dad said to the counterpart.

"She did it," said Maj's "twin." "It's in the computer if you want to look at it."

"Oh, please," her dad said, more than effectively mimicking her. "I believe in calculus, but I don't need to go look at it . . . not that much anyway. Maj, Mom asked if when you're done, you would take a moment to look around in her workspace and find her that recipe for the marzipan *lebkuchen* again. She's elbow-deep in Nana Do's fruitcake recipe at the moment, and she doesn't want to go on-line."

Maj shook her head and smiled. This was certainly a safer place to be, at the moment, than the kitchen was. "I will. You going out now?"

"In a little while. Have fun, honey."

"Will do, Daddy."

Her father's head vanished, making Maj grin harder for a moment as she thought thoughts of the Great and Powerful Oz, whom her dad was beginning to resemble as his hairline continued to recede.

Her mother, who sometimes more closely resembled the absent-minded professor than her father did, was another story entirely. When she was not designing and setting up computer systems for people, and making what Maj suspected was a fair amount of money at it, she was also one of those people who cook for pleasure, and who do bizarre and amazing things that no one else in their right mind would do.

In her mother's case, as the holiday season started its slow approach, this meant making tons of fruitcake to give as gifts, and building gingerbread "houses"—though perhaps "houses" was the wrong word. She had replicated buildings of Frank Lloyd Wright's in gingerbread, including the famous "Glass House," which featured sugar-glass windows that she cast herself because "no one else gets them flat enough."

It was from her mom that Maj had first caught the simming

bug . . . though her mom's sims ranged so widely through so many media that Maj sometimes came away from them shaking her head.

She shook her head now. "Remind me to pick up that structural gingerbread recipe later," she said. "Now where was I?"

"The meatball," said Maj's doppelgänger.

Maj looked over at the artificial "horizon" indicator, a sphere set in a surrounding sphere of clear liquid, and pressed the "home" button. It homed and settled itself into the lines that indicated that the aircraft was presently sitting flat and level. She glanced over to see her counterpart doing the same thing with the duplicate meatball on the copilot's side.

"On," Maj's duplicate said. "ADS engine operations—"

"Amplitude gauges OK."

"Fuel tank pressurization sequence—"

"One through eight OK."

"We've got people out on the tarmac," Maj's duplicate suddenly said.

"Huh?" Maj was surprised at that. She had programmed her playroom to let her know with an audible chime when someone entered. She hitched herself up a little and peered over the edge of the cockpit. Roddy L'Officier was wandering around out there, hugging himself and generally making "brr" gestures.

"You're early," she shouted at him. "Go away and come back in fifteen minutes."

"It's OK," Roddy said. "I'll just wander around."

"Fine," Maj said, and added under her breath as she sat back down again, "Go ahead, freeze your butt off, I don't care."

She spent a moment trying to rerail her derailed train of thought. It took a moment. Of all the members of the simming group she worked with, she was least fond of Roddy. He was one of those people who seemed to consider it their place in life to be a seemingly never-ending trial to those around them. He was nothing special to look at: dark-haired, a little short, a little pudgy with the kind of "baby fat" that some people were late growing out of, especially if they liked junk food a lot. But Roddy was a boaster, a real in-your-face type, brilliant and never shy about reminding you of the fact, always acting like he was in control, or secretly knowledgeable about everything that was going on around him, always shoving himself and his advice into your business, whether they were wanted or not.

Maj generally did her best to ignore him. She didn't exchange friendly virt-mails with him, as she did with most of the rest of the group. He sent enough of them to her, though, sitting back in an unusually fancy implant-support chair and passing judgment on her sims in his whiny, superior voice, even several months after a given run-through, and generally telling her what he thought she should do to make them "acceptable." *To* him *maybe,* Maj thought. *Picky little creep. He's plainly mistaken me for someone who gives a flying fart about what he thinks.*

Then she took a deep breath. Maj had a temper, and sometimes it got the better of her . . . which embarrassed her. Doubtless Roddy had good reasons for being the way he was. For one thing, he would never discuss his family. Maj suspected there was difficulty of some kind at home. *Not my business,* she thought as she continued to work her way down the lengthy checklist, though she had to wonder about someone who had such expensive clothes on all the time, the newest Barrington slicks and HueElls, while at the same time never seemed to have enough money for the occasional group outings for a pizza. *Odd, but . . . who* knows *what's going on with him.*

And it had to be said that though his manner was routinely a pain, he did occasionally—*more than occasionally,* Maj thought, forcing herself to be honest—come up with useful suggestions regarding sims. He really was very good at them. *If only he could make the suggestions without making it sound like he was some saintly charitable genius type with a mission to the brain-dead,* Maj thought.

"More visitors," said her counterpart.

"Oh, frack, I don't believe this," Maj muttered, and sat up again. There were three more people down there, easily. *What's the matter with that chime? I've got to check the code, something's gone south. . . .* "Can't any of you tell time?" she shouted down at the newcomers. "I'm still doing my preflight checks! Come back a little later!"

"Don't mind us, we'll just walk around," said Bob's cheerful voice from somewhere directly underneath Maj. "Hey, wow, look at this. . . ."

She had to smile at that, just slightly. Bob was not normally effusive in his praise, and seemed to be trying to hold a poker face in place all the time . . . but Maj suspected that was because he was permanently excited about most things, and for some while now had been cultivating the ability to hide the fact.

"Madeline, can't you turn the temperature up out here a little?" came another shout from below. That was Mairead, comfort-loving and intolerant of conditions as always. Maj remembered with amusement how bitterly she had complained to Bob about the "air pollution" from the cannons at Gettysburg.

"Sorry, Mair," Maj yelled back, "it's the high desert at the end of September. What do you expect, the beach?"

"But deserts are hot!"

"Not at night," someone else remarked from further back under the plane: Shih Chin's voice. "Make yourself a jacket and keep quiet. I'm pacing."

Maj smiled. Chin was the kind of person who had to know exactly how big something was. If she was pacing the long way down the Valkyrie, that would keep her busy for a few minutes. "Crap," Maj said to her counterpart. "I forgot where we were."

"TACAN."

"On," Maj said, frowning. There was only one TACAN system in the plane, which was a serious pain in the butt as far as Maj was concerned. In those early days before global positioning satellites, being able to figure out where you were was vital, and TACAN helped you do that . . . but for those purposes, two systems, or three, were better than one. Apparently the Air Force upper-ups had felt that their XB-70 pilots were incapable of getting lost, or if they did, that they could darn well pull out a map and read it.

Or stop at a gas station and ask for directions, Maj thought. *Idiots.* But everybody had been trying to save money. What should have been a whole program's worth of aircraft was now going to be just three, and NASA and the Air Force were determined to wring every last penny's worth of high-Mach research out of them. An extra TACAN system, at that point, probably looked like a needless extravagance. . . .

"Next!" Maj's counterpart said. "Come on, get your brains in order. Your nerves are showing."

"Never," said Maj . . . but she smiled a one-sided smile as she went back to the preflights. "Test recording . . ."

"Digital on. Analog on."

"Air-induction-control system." It was one of the most crucial parts of the aircraft, the ramps inside the air intakes that would expand and contract to manipulate the airflow to the engines.

"All ramps answering."

"Lateral bobweight."

"Normal."

"Flight display."

"To pilot . . ."

"Command control."

"To pilot."

Maj watched her copilot throw the last toggle. "That it?"

"That's everything but the shouting."

"Great."

She stood up, stretched a little, shivered in the cold, then carefully started going down the ladder again. The sky, which had been flushing through ever more outrageous shades of peach and rose, now suddenly paled in the space of a breath or two to a thin, faint, clear gold as the first limb of the sun came molten and blazing over the low jagged mountains at the edge of the world.

As she got to the bottom and jumped down, the others' virtual presences gathered around her. Bob, looking skeptical as usual; Mairead, shaking her blazing red curls in bemusement at the big wing she looked up at; and all the others, walking back to her from down the length of the plane, touching the parts of it that they were tall enough to reach . . . which in this case was only the landing gear, big enough to dwarf everyone in the group.

Mere size, of course, was not going to be enough to impress *this* bunch. Maj remembered the scorn that had been rained on Chin's simulation of the heavy-lifter *Arcturus* . . . though it had deserved it, since its wheels had fallen off halfway through the simulation. A bumping noise got her attention, and Maj turned and saw Roddy actually kicking the Valk's tires. "Hey—!" she said, and then stopped. Why be petty about it? The chocks were held in place by the simulation, and it wasn't as if he could do anything to the tires anyway. They were built to handle landings of a half-million-pound plane at a 150 miles an hour.

Not that they always did, her uneasy memory said, but that wasn't her problem right this second. The group gathered around her, and Maj gestured upward and said, "The XB-70 Valkyrie."

Kelly pointed up toward the left side of the hull just under the cockpit, where elegantly scrolled letters said *Rosweisse.* "What's that?"

"Her name," Maj said, and was unable to keep herself from flushing a little with embarrassment.

" 'White Rose'? " There was laughter. "What kind of name is that for a Valkyrie?"

"One of the first ones," Maj said. "Go check the *Elder Edda.* Wagner used the name . . . but only because the Norse used it first. They didn't see why you couldn't have a delicate little pretty-flower name and still be perfectly able to kill things." She gave Kelly a slightly more challenging look than usual. "Anyway, it beats calling a submarine *Indomitable* when all it does is blow itself up."

Kelly suddenly looked rather more interested in the landing gear than he had been, and Maj immediately felt guilty for making fun of him. "Well," said Chin in her even-handed sort of way, "performance is something we haven't evaluated yet. Let's look her over."

The group set out on their own walk-round, and Maj went around with them, trying to look at *Rosweisse* as if she had never seen the plane before. *The wheels,* she thought as they went past the landing gear, *that blown tire* . . . and then she forcibly put the worry aside for the moment. There was nothing she could do about the tires just now, though they would be enough of a challenge shortly. Maj had dedicated herself to building the plane exactly as its designers had, with all their bugs in place . . . and working to find out what could have been done to make it function anyway, something that the vacillating government of that time had not been willing to do. It was a private pet peeve, and if Maj could make it work, it would be a tiny *I-told-you-so* to the world in general and the bureaucrats in particular. Eventually, when she had wrung every last bit of performance out of the simulator, Maj was determined to send it to the brains at NASA/Dryden, that now included the facility that had once been Muroc/Edwards AFB, and let them see what they could make of her data.

There was, of course, no hope of Maj's findings doing the Valkyrie itself any good, for it would never fly again. The only remaining one, AV-1, stood silent and thoughtful at the Modern Aviation hangar at the Air Force Museum at Wright Patterson, a faint air of tragedy and sorrow hanging about her. She was the last of her line, for her younger sister, AV-2, had somehow been bumped by a F-104 Starfighter doing chase-plane duty on her forty-first flight. With the stabilizers torn off one wing by the collision, she could not be saved from the inverted flat spin that ensued. She'd crashed, killing one of her two pilots who was unable to eject in time. And before that had happened, AV-3 had been stillborn, her funding axed before she was built.

Together, for Maj, the three aircraft drew a picture of tremendous potential that, due to bad luck, shortsightedness, and a design too advanced for that time's materials technology, had never been realized. You could sit and mourn that lost potential and do nothing more about it, or you could rebuild it, and get it as right as it could have been gotten, and offer the result up on the altar of possibilities yet to come. "Doing something," her mother had said to her one evening, passing through the simulation on her way to a meeting to pick up some recipes, "matters . . . even when it doesn't seem to."

"It's a lot bigger than a Blackbird," said Sander as the group paused under the towering twin tail, fifty feet above their heads at its top, and now blazing in the early sunshine. He had done a Blackbird sim some while back, and it had been a lovely one, mimicking the graceful old plane right down to the way it sat on the tarmac and leaked fuel out its joints before the heat of supersonic flight "grew" the plane a foot longer and into its proper shape. Flight crews had given it some rude names because of this habit. All Maj knew was that she kept smelling Avtur for about a week after spending time in that sim with Sander and the others. *It was probably psychosomatic,* she kept telling herself, much preferring that idea to the thought that her brain was starting to lose the ability to tell the difference between real and virtual experience.

"The fuel it carries," Maj said, "weighs as much as the Blackbird did, just by itself. She was designed for situations where they didn't feel they could count on midair refueling." *Because civilization might already have been destroyed in the exchange of missiles . . .*

They all walked on, down around the tail and up the other side. The frost was already vanishing off the tarmac as they left, leaving only the occasional wet patch where it had been particularly thick. The sun glanced off that single coat of white paint, blazing. The needle nose was almost invisible in the bright day from this angle. Maj hoped they could see what she saw . . . that the Valkyrie was just a desperately cool plane.

One of the things that had attracted Maj to the XB-70, besides the plane's fraught history, was simply how beautiful she was. She had the look of the old SSTs that were (in a way) her children: that same long, straight, patrician needle nose that dropped for landing, and the slender body and huge graceful delta wing reminiscent of the better-known Concordes. Maj had fallen in love with those old passenger planes long ago, even though they had been in retirement for years, and when she had accidentally discovered this discarded, lovely stepmother to their line, she had sworn to simulate it properly. The discovery that the plane had been trouble to its designers from the word "go" had only made Maj more determined to make her fly again.

Commercial aviation had gone in far different directions, taking up again another nearly lost heritage, the flying wing. Now huge subsonic lifting-body-based craft, Boeing-MDD's replacements for the old 747's, routinely and economically carried thousands of people at once to their destinations; and the much faster and much more expensive hypersonic suborbital craft—aerospace planes—had made their debut a few years back, in their design and general looks more stepchildren of the Space Shuttle than of the XB-70. None of them, though, had the elegance, the cachet, of the Valkyrie . . . at least not to Maj's mind. And it looked like some of the others agreed with her.

"Those are some wings," Fergal said.

"They keep them straight for takeoff and landing," Maj said. "But they flex down at the tips, about a third of the way down—about twenty-five degrees for speeds between 300 knots and Mach one-point-four, and then down to sixty-five degrees for the run up to Mach three. They're the largest movable aerodynamic device ever used . . . twenty feet wide at the trailing edge."

"Very impressive," Roddy said in that slightly sneering voice that meant he might be impressed but wasn't going to show it.

Maj ignored him. They stopped again beside the cockpit ladder. "She's a nice one," said Sander.

" 'She,' " Roddy said, his voice mocking.

"What else? Ships and planes are always she," Maj said calmly. "Call them 'he' and they crash and burn. Not an opinion, just the truth. 'You can't have opinions about the truth. . . .' " It was a favorite quote of her dad's, attributed to some dead musician.

Roddy snorted and turned away. "Okay," Sander said. "We've all read the code. We've seen the craft, and physically she matches your stats—that's plain. So what're you going to do?"

"I'm going to do what they did the first time out," Maj said. "Take her up and see how she does."

"You're not going to break the sound barrier?"

"Chicken," Roddy said, and began to cluck.

Fergal looked at Roddy coolly. "Revealing your true colors again, are you, our Roderick?" Fergal's Yorkshire accent went broader than usual. Maj got the feeling, as she occasionally had before, that Fergal didn't care much for Roddy either.

"Rhode Island Red," Maj said. "As for not going supersonic, *au contraire, mon vieux Sandre.* I intend to take her to Mach two and hold her there for what they later referred to as a 'heat soak'—some of the parts never really functioned correctly until they'd had time to settle into their proper shapes at the kind of high heat you get from running supersonic for prolonged periods. Naturally, she will give me trouble when I try this. She gave them trouble too. But I believe I can handle it better than they did."

"Didn't the landing gear burn up?"

"Not quite," Maj said. "There was a pressure surge in the brake system. It locked the rear wheels of the left-side main gear, and the tires caught fire. I think that was due to a mismanagement of one of the hydraulic systems. I'm going to see if I can correct it this time out."

"Where's our focus?" Fergal said. Normally when you had a number of people preparing to experience a simulation all together, and when the simming area was cramped, you elected a "focus" point from which they would appear to experience it.

"Back of the cockpit," Maj said, "as if against the end of the canopy. There'll also be a secondary focus in one of the chase planes."

Very suddenly, and Maj hoped showily, they appeared on the tarmac as they were mentioned: a threesome of F-104 Starfighters, their brushed chrome gleaming blindingly in the sun and their engines already wound up and screaming with mechanical enthusiasm. Everyone winced and covered their ears. Maj flushed again with embarrassment. She had forgotten to turn the environmental sound down; it had been so quiet before dawn. She said, "Down sixty decibels, please." The environment obliged her, and the triple scream of the Starfighters backed itself down to a trio of elegant laryngitic whispers.

"So," Maj said, "if you all want to make yourselves comfortable . . ."

Eight chairs of wildly varying kinds appeared well away from the Valkyrie, and the Group of Seven went off to settle themselves in them. Maj found herself standing there alone, and feeling, for the first time this morning, somewhat scared.

Why? There's nothing to be scared of. . . .

Except that she hated not getting things right . . . especially in front of people. And if anything went wrong with this—

She breathed in, breathed out, and turned back to the ladder, which was now wet and slick with the melted frost. As she put her hands on the rung at eye level to start climbing, Maj thought, *This really* is *a good simulation. They won't be able to see how much my hands are sweating. . . .*

2

She settled herself into the left-hand seat, breathed in, breathed out again, and started doing up the six-point restraints. Her counterpart had already done this.

"Engine start?" said Maj Two.

"Start the list," said Maj.

"Final fuel weight—"

"One hundred thirty-two thousand pounds."

"Nose ramp—"

"Down."

"Flap position—"

"To auto."

"Wing-tip fold—"

"To auto."

"Engine number one start."

"Starting."

The whine, the sudden shudder through the airframe, never failed to catch her by surprise—it was the concentrated sound of rising adrenaline, and she could actually feel it at both sides of her middle back, a rush of paradoxical heat. *Rosweisse* was alive. "Fuel mix—"

"Full and rich."

"Hydraulic pressure—"

"Primary system is coming up."

Maj was astonished at how dry her mouth was getting. *It's not like I haven't been through this before,* she thought. *But some sims are less simulated than others, I guess*—

"Flap pos," she said, and it came out strangled.

Her other self laughed—possibly the wisest response under the circumstances, and certainly something Maj would have done herself if she were calmer. *Well, I just* did *it myself. Oh, never mind!*

"Full play, position to auto," Maj Two said.

"Rudder—"

"Full play, position to auto."

"Engine one heat?"

"She's on the line."

"Good. Engine number two start."

"Starting. Mix rich and full—"

The whole aircraft shuddered with the torque of the quick-start sequence, the far starboard-side engine whining into life and the whine rapidly becoming a scream balancing the yell to port. "Mach repeaters—"

"At zero-point-zero . . . Alert!" said Maj Two as a subdued squawking started in the cockpit. "Failure in number two engine's cooling loop."

"Shut down and restart." This was in the original flight. Maj had not yet tracked the cause of this particular problem to its lair, and there was nothing to do but run the simulation "around" it. Fortunately, the problem had not affected anything important in reality.

Maj Two shut down the number-two engine, and she and Maj started to wait the mandated two minutes. Down on the tarmac, Maj could see some heads craning as people not yet riding inside the cockpit at the "focus" started wondering what was going on. From behind her, though, Fergal's voice said, "You change your mind, Mads?"

"It's in the schedule," Maj said, with only slight annoyance. "Check the code. Restart?"

"Restarting."

The shudder came again, and the engine came up screaming. This time the note it sang was steady. "Time check?"

"Seven fourteen."

"Perfect. Engine three start."

"Starting. Rich and full—"

"Engine four—"

"Starting—"

"Canopy," Maj said, and her counterpart reached over and hit the toggle. The shudder repeated once with each engine, the scream scaled up even through the cockpit's sealing, and the sound of it changed a little as the cockpit pressurized. Maj swallowed, swallowed again. Her ears popped.

"That everything?" she said to Maj Two.

"Nothing left but to roll."

"Let's roll then," Maj said, gripping the yoke. "Chocks away."

The chocks vanished. Slowly, an inch, two inches, five, a foot, *Rosweisse* rolled forward and began to gain speed.

"Muroc Control, this is AV/1," Maj said. She always smiled a little when she called them. "Control" was a single tin shed with a radio and a bored duty officer. "On the apron, for taxiway one zero."

"Air Vehicle One, you are clear for taxi on one zero to active four left, cleared to take off at your discretion," said the dry voice—yet another purveyor of the worldwide air-traffic-control accent, the same middle-pitched easygoing drawl wherever you went.

"Roger, Muroc Control, thank you very much and good day," Maj said, and was glad she had nothing else to say. Her mouth felt dryer than the whole Mojave Desert around her. She swallowed one more time, a fairly hopeless business—there was no spit left in her.

Maj concentrated on taxiing, which was more than enough of a problem. This early in the Valkyrie's development, no one had yet figured out why she was such a beast to taxi. Her front gear in particular developed a terrible and violent chatter at low speeds, which meant that it took hundreds of feet to brake at speeds as low as five miles an hour. For the moment, all Maj could do was set her teeth, which her counterpart was doing as well, to judge by the strained look on her face. "End of one zero coming up," said Maj Two after a moment, her voice wobbling amusingly with the wobbling of the aircraft.

"Left turn and turnaround at the end of four," Maj said. Her counterpart nodded. They had been through this part of the drill often enough.

They wobbled and wobbled and *wobbled* as the turn came

up. "Did they *ever* figure out what this problem was?" said Alain from "behind" them.

"Not that I know of," Maj said. "I think all the pilots needed dentures after they retired from flying this plane."

Maj cranked the yoke around as they came to the turn. The wobbling got much worse, as it always did, and then slightly better as they straightened out. It was a longish run down to the end of the runway, but not one of the watching simmers spoke. They were all used to prolonged quiet periods in some simulations, since all too many great events consisted of periods of frantic action interspersed with much longer periods of mind-dulling inactivity.

"Let's bring her around," Maj said to Maj Two at last. The two of them hauled on the yokes together; the Valkyrie had a poor turning circle, and her hydraulics were not at their best when working inside such a tight radius. After a few minutes, taking their time—for Maj had no intention of making the plane wobble any worse than it was already doing—they lined up on four left and sat still a moment.

Maj looked down the long silvery expanse of dried salt pan reaching away before them. Even this early in the morning, heat was beginning to shimmer down the length of it, a silvery curtain through which the distant dun-and-beige mountains wavered indistinct and unreal.

"Time check," Maj said.

"Eight twenty-four."

"Sounds good to me," Maj said, for that was exactly the time when the test flight in question had begun her takeoff roll. She reached to her right for the six throttles, folded her hand around them, and made sure of her grip—they were a handful. "Ready?"

"Ready!"

Was that other voice sounding a little dry, a little squeaky, as well? Maj grinned, and shoved the throttles forward to the pre-afterburner maximum.

Rosweisse started to roll. The wobbling got much worse— then slowly as she picked up speed, it got less, then suddenly went away altogether. "Ten knots," said Maj Two. "Fifteen. Twenty—"

Maj swallowed, hopelessly, one last time, watching the

ground-speed indicator and airspeed indicator inch upward in tandem. "Forty. Fifty—"

The scream of the engines blotted out the rumble of the runway now. The slightest change to the feel of the aircraft had already started, that lightening, the sense that she wanted to be up, *would* be up, any second now—she was fighting with gravity, and winning. "One hundred knots. One-ten—one-twenty—one-fifty—"

"Vee one," Maj said, watching the silvery baked mud-salt surface pour past them, too fast for her to focus on anything further away than fifty feet or so. Joshua trees flicked past like broken-armed stick figures as the aircraft passed stall speed and continued to accelerate, those big wings biting the wind now, the craft bucking a little as the pre-takeoff turbulence started to build over the airfoil. Only the mountains ahead and to the sides seemed to remain unmoving. "One-seventy—"

Maj tried to swallow and failed. "Coming up on rotate," she said, and tightened her grip on the yoke.

"One-ninety. Vee two—"

"Rotating," Maj said, and pulled back, watching the angle-of-attack meter closely. Too sharp and *Rosweisse* would flip over; she'd tried to do that before—"AOA nine degrees—"

The nose started to lift. There was a sudden decrease of noise behind them as the nose gear, far behind them, lifted free of the ground. The yoke shook in Maj's hands. She held it steady as her seat seemed to tilt back and the front of the cockpit window filled with hard blue sky. "Two hundred—"

—and then came a kind of sudden bound, and the runway rumble was simply gone entirely. Nothing remained but the scream of the engines far behind, and a relentless, wonderful pushing in the small of Maj's back as the Valkyrie lifted into the air and soared up away from the runway. Trans-sonic vapor erupted in the airstream over the Valkyrie's wing-roots, the vapor streaming out behind her in broad, flat twin plumes that instantly tattered away in the back blast from the engines.

"Two-oh-five," said Maj Two.

"Roj that," Maj said. They were matching the original flight in all important particulars so far. "Turning right out of pattern. I'm going for altitude."

"Roj. Two-fifty now. Nose coming up on auto."

"Up and locked. Come up to three-ten and hold her there."
Maj stepped on the rudder pedal as the plane's "droop snoot"
came up and locked into place, then turned the yoke and pulled
back. Both engines answered instantly and with ease. There
was such a profound difference between the way this aircraft
handled on the ground—like an overweight cow—and the
way it flew. As she turned, Maj looked out of the canopy and
saw the chase planes following her without too much difficulty. Later, though, she would give them a run for their
money.

"Altitude fifteen hundred now," she said for the recorders
(and for the audience, invisible behind her or out in one of
the chase planes, the F-104 that hung closest off her port side).
"Wing tips to twenty-five degrees."

"On auto. They've done it."

"Good. Muroc, fifteen heading for one five-zero."

"AV/1, roger, cleared to one-five-zero."

She pushed the throttles into afterburner full, and headed
westward over the dry lake bed, gaining altitude fast, the Valkyrie beginning to show her mettle now. "Climbs like a bat,
this one," Sander said.

"You ain't seen nothing yet," Maj said. "We'll make fifteen
thousand feet in about ten seconds. She likes to climb . . . it's
the camber on those wings, and the compression wave." Indeed Maj was having to exert some control to keep the craft
from climbing *too* steeply—*Rosweisse*'s response to the pull
on the yoke was almost overeager when the afterburners were
at full. That "eagerness to please" had often tempted Maj
to find out firsthand whether the Valkyrie could execute
the lean-over-backwards-and-fly-tail-first "cobra" maneuver
made so famous by the old Sukhois. There was no question
that *Rosweisse* could manage the necessary accelerations, but
the airframe strength was a question mark. Either way, Maj
didn't want to try it, on purpose or accidentally, on *this* run.

She backed the throttles down a little, but *Rosweisse* didn't
care—she plunged upward, shouldering the air out of the way.
"Hull temp going up," said Maj Two, glancing out and back
over her shoulder to see if she could catch sight of the idio-

syncratic "dimpling" that the skin sometimes showed at such times. "One-eighty F now."

"Sounds good. Accelerating," said Maj. "Still climbing. Passing through one five zero. Muroc, AV/1 through one-five-zero, heading for three-zero-zero."

"Cleared for three-zero-zero, AV/1."

"Hull at two hundred F," said Maj Two, looking out and down into the blue day. The high desert was spreading itself out beneath them like an increasingly distant dun-colored carpet.

"Two hundred's good," Maj said. "Wing tips to sixty-five degrees."

"They're down."

"Out of four hundred knots for five. Four-fifty—five hundred—"

The speed was pouring on now. Maj was being pushed back into her seat. She loved it. *It would be too tacky to play the "Ride" now,* she thought, and grinned. Yet enough times, when she had flown this sim by herself, she had done it, reveling in the way the scream of the engines went with the mad crash of Wagner's "Ride of the Valkyries," the full version with the vocals in place, all the shouting and the high notes and the *ho-yo-to-ho*s. This ferocious creature, lancing irresistibly through the high winds of the upper stratosphere, sometimes producing flickers of lightning from static discharge as she pierced through the clouds at lower altitudes, was a perfect evocation of her namesakes: swift, deadly, but at the same time there was something joyous about her, about the way she went. Once again Maj wished that the Valkyrie had been built in numbers, so that people who needed a weapon to use in a righteous cause could have had her to use . . . and the rest of the time to fly in for joy: though precious few pilots would admit that kind of pleasure to any but one of their own number. *Ho-yo-to-ho,* Maj thought, and eased the throttles forward just a little bit more.

"Five-fifty," Maj Two said. "Six hundred. Six-fifty." A slight shuddering started, but nothing serious. The XB-70 had only a little of the difficulty with near-presonic flight that her smaller, lower-digit cousin X's did, partly because she was so much more massive, partly because the compression wave rad-

ically changed the shape of the pre/postsonic "bowshock."
"Seven hundred. What's the air temperature?"

"Thirty-three below F."

"Here it comes then. Seven hundred thirty-three—"

There were two distinct *BLAM!*s as the bowshock rolled
down the Valkyrie's body. Inside the cockpit the shuddering
stopped, and things got quieter still, the engine noise seeming
somewhat diminished, and the hum or rush of noise transmit-
ted directly by the airframe seeming louder by comparison.
"Mach one," Maj said. "One-point-two—"

A subdued cheer came from a couple of the voices riding
in the "focus" behind her. "Oh, come on," Maj said, "even
things with wheels can go *that* fast. Now, though—"

She eased forward on the throttles again. With the sound
barrier out of the way, acceleration got easier—it was as if the
aircraft had originally been traveling in water, and had suddenly leapt into the air. *This is her element,* Maj thought, *this
is what she was made for . . . life above Mach 1.* "One-point-
three," she said. "One-point-five—"

An alarm went off. Maj's head snapped around, and her
heart started pounding. That was *not* one of the alarms which
had occurred in the original flight; nothing was supposed to
happen until—

"Got a red light," Maj Two said, sounding as concerned
as Maj was. "AICS malfunction."

"What kind?" Maj hung on to the yoke. The plane wasn't
doing anything bad yet anyway—

"Ramp malfunction. They're not contracting. Intakes two
and three—"

"What're the revs?"

"Two is showing a hundred and eight percent."

That *was* in the original flight. They had shut that engine
down when it started to over-rev. "Kill it," Maj said. "See
if that does anything for the ramps in three."

Maj Two reached out and pulled the throttle for engine two
slowly back down to "cold," then threw its master toggle.
Something went out of the engine note, half a tone's worth of
harmony, and the Valkyrie bounced a little. That was to be
expected, as the changed pressure-wave configuration asserted

itself down the length of the aircraft. ''What's three doing
now?''

Another alarm, louder this time. ''No good,'' Maj Two said.
''And there goes ramp four. Ramp five—''

Maj flushed hot, not with embarrassment this time. The Valkyrie was beginning to vibrate, the shaking building toward
the kind of severe vibration they had been experiencing on the
ground—except they were *not* on the ground. She reached for
the throttles and started easing them back—and then started
to feel the unresponsiveness in the yoke.

Trouble. Big trouble. And none of it anything from the original flight. All *that* she would have been prepared for. . . .

''Flameout in one!'' Maj Two said, urgent. ''Six is losing
through-put—''

BANG! BANG! said the air outside the Valkyrie. She was
going subsonic, catastrophically so, not under control as she
did it. The nose pitched forward, and further forward, further
still. Maj pulled back on the yoke, couldn't stop it—

'' 'I say, Number One, my end is diving . . . what the hell
is *your* end doing?' '' From back in the ''focus'' it came, a
remark attributed to one of the K-boat commanders that Kelly
had invoked during his last run-through of his sim. It had
become a joke in the Group of Seven, a running gag suggesting that something unexpected was happening. Right now it
was the last thing that Maj wanted to hear. She said a word
that would have annoyed her mother, and kept pulling on the
yoke. ''Three's gone,'' Maj Two shouted, as the plane plunged
earthward. ''Five's gone—''

The ground was spinning far below Maj like an old-
fashioned CD in its player. Except that it was not below her,
it was *above* her, visible through the ceiling of the canopy.
And it was starting to get closer. She and her counterpart and
the Valkyrie were on their backs, falling, spinning around the
aircraft's central axis. Inverted flat spin, the worst kind, almost
nothing she could do, no way to recover—

Almost. Maj pushed the yoke straight forward, held it there
though it fought in her hands like a cat squirming to get away
from her. *Oh, no, you don't,* she thought, and hung on like
grim death while the yoke bucked and jumped and tried to
crawl out of her grip. Across the cockpit, her counterpart was

doing the same. "Meatball's going nuts—" she yelled.

"How can it help it? Pull, help me pull—"

The spin gaining some angle now, but slowly, excruciatingly slowly, as the nose began to pitch slowly, slowly down, and the spin started to increase speed. Maj desperately wanted to throw up, and was grateful that she had had no time to eat anything this afternoon. "Disallow Gs!" she shouted at the simulation, and it listened to her, canceling out the increasing assault of simulated centripetal force that would shortly have left her unconscious, all the blood centrifuged to one side or the other of her brain, or right out of it down into her trunk. Maj shook her head until her vision put itself right again, and concentrated on the furious power of the yoke trying to tear itself out of her hands, meanwhile trying to ignore how bruised her arms and shoulders were feeling.

I say, Number One, my end is diving. . . . Not funny now. Not at all. She pulled the yoke to her as hard as she could. From a spin in two dimensions there was little chance of recovering. From a straight downward spin—the odds got slightly better. If you could stop the spin, that is, and turn it into a straightforward dive. From that you could pull up. *If the altimeter's forgiving, that is.* At the moment, it said 21000 and was racing backwards at about a thousand feet a second. *Less than half a minute.* She pulled at the yoke as it if was the reins of some particularly mouth-hardened recalcitrant trail-ride jade, some horse with no nerves and no brains, and stood on the rudder pedals as if standing up in the stirrups—

The angle deepened. The sickening spinning of the view out through the canopy turned into one even more upsetting, half-ground, half-sky, with an uneasy wobble like a top running out of spin. *Come on,* Maj thought as she pulled, *come on—* She wanted to see nothing but that dun-colored ground ahead of her. That she could deal with. The hydraulics were still answering, the rudder pedals were stiff but workable. And another part of her mind was saying, *Make sure we're still over the lakes. Don't drop this in the middle of somewhere where there might be people—*

She pushed at the pedals and hauled at the yoke. *Just dirt now. Just the spin. Counterclockwise. Okay. Left rudder, left only—*

18000, 17000, 16000, said the altimeter, cutting her very little slack. The ground bloomed out wider, the sky retreated behind her as Maj pulled and pulled. Finally the ground completely filled the forward view. That was exactly what she wanted. "Here goes," she said to her counterpart, and came down with both feet on the left rudder pedal.

Nothing—

—nothing—

14000. 13000. 12000—

"Bail out!" yelled Maj Two.

"Not an option," Maj said. *It's only a simulation. You can't die in a simulation. And I am* not *going to let this go down the tubes this way.* She stood on that rudder pedal for all she was worth, and held the yoke steady, held it hard, pointed it straight down the center of the spinning tunnel the Valkyrie seemed to be drilling toward the ground. No sky anymore. Only ground, but the spin was slowing—

—10000. 9000, 8000, 7000, 6000—

—slowing. *Come on, come on, snap out of it—*

The spin was slowing, but not enough. There was not enough time. They would crash. From across the cockpit, her counterpart threw her a single despairing look. It was not an expression Maj liked seeing on her own face, however genuine it was. And it was genuine.

—4000, 3000—

At 2800 feet the left wing gave—at the tip first, and then at the root. Revolutionary though its design might have been, it was never meant to cope with stresses like these. The spin went uncontrolled again. Maj set her teeth and hung on to the yoke. Nothing else to do—

The loss of the wing paradoxically slowed the fall a fraction, flattening the spin out again, so that Maj had just enough time to see the altimeter say *1000,* and then—

Black. Everything was simply black for a moment. All Maj could hear was the crazy pounding of her own heart. Then the world "came on" again, her playroom's view defaulting to what the chase-plane saw. Far below was what at first glance seemed a little fire, a brushfire, out among the Joshua trees. Except it was not a brushfire, for no brush on earth made such huge flame-shot billows of black smoke. The Valkyrie had still been nearly fully loaded when she went down. It would be a long while yet before that much Avtur burned away.

The background default asserted itself then, her playroom's computer having noticed that the central item of her simulation had "ceased to exist" in this run. Maj found herself standing a mile or so from the crash, where the Valkyrie had been parked before dawn, and rising from their chairs, the other members of the Group of Seven were coming over to her.

She stood and watched them come, trying hard to calm her breathing down as they came across the tarmac. Their expressions varied widely. Tall, dark Bob looked completely nonplussed, as if he'd seen the moon fall down; Mairead's vibrant good looks had a ruffled look, her eyebrows knitted in either confusion or annoyance; Fergal's broad face was a study of someone caught between amusement that he wasn't going to reveal and an expression of pure rue. Kelly looked resigned, as much to Maj's own failure as to his own recent ones. Sander looked pissed off, not at Maj, but at Alain, who by his looks plainly thought this whole thing was a riot. Chin's face revealed nothing at all. Roddy—

Maj swallowed one last time. They were drawing near, the group of people her own age whose opinions—at least on this subject—she valued more than anyone else's . . . and in front of whom she had royally and completely fracked up.

They gathered around her.

"What *was* that?" Chin said.

Maj shook her head. "I don't know. An accident."

"Or something wrong with your code," said Alain, still grinning.

She would have loved an excuse to wipe that grin off him, but that was not her style. Instead she said, "You might have had the grace to point it out then, a problem that big, unless *you* didn't see it either."

Alain blinked.

"Did anyone see anything in Maj's code that might have caused a major blowup like that?" Chin said.

A lot of shaken heads . . . but Maj noticed that Roddy was holding very still, watching the others' reactions.

"It's a really complex simulation," Fergal said, giving Maj credit for that much at least. "There are a ton of things that could have gone wrong with it. And the real thing always threw all kinds of problems at its pilots, didn't it?''

"It did," Maj said, "but nothing like that."

"So you have no idea of what went wrong."

She shook her head, feeling like a complete fume-brain as she stood there in the warm September sunshine.

Kelly sighed. "Well," he said, and looked at the others. "We can't grade her on this one."

"Why not?" Alain demanded.

Maj looked at him and kept her thoughts to herself, most forcibly. Alain the good-looking, Alain the good-natured, Alain the suave talker who rarely let his real thoughts about anything out. Except occasionally, at which time you tended to find that you had been completely wrong about them. "She put her sim up for evaluation," Alain said. "It failed miserably. Shouldn't that be counted as just what happened?"

"The Group didn't make it count for me," Kelly said, "when *K12* blew all those holes open and sank itself. Catastrophic failure . . . but the composition software turned out to be buggy. How do we know it wasn't something like that? We should at least check."

Looks were exchanged around the group. "It's a point," Fergal said. "Maj, you want to look into it?"

"I don't think anyone should look into anything but that," Alain said, jerking a thumb over his shoulder at the black smoke rising a mile away. He looked at the others.

So did Fergal. "Anybody else share Alain's views?" he said.

More glances were exchanged. Mairead shook her head. So did Chin and Bob and Sander.

Maj sighed. *Small mercies,* she thought. But she noticed again how still Roddy had been keeping himself.

"That's a majority," Fergal said. "Mads, better take that code home and have a good look at it. We'll run through it again with you when you're ready."

"Right," Maj said. "Thanks."

Several of them sighed then, and looked out at the smoke rising.

And Roddy looked at Maj, the first direct look he'd given

her. "Well," Roddy said. "I hope you've learned your lesson."

She looked at him in complete bemusement. "What? What lesson?"

"To be a little more careful with your code. If you let people tamper with it . . . bad things can happen. Unexpected things. But then you're not very good at expecting the unexpected."

"I don't have the slightest clue what you're talking about," Maj said, turning away from him, "and since half the time you don't either, that makes us about even." She was in no mood for his snide comments at the moment. "Anyway, if you're not going to deliver useful criticism, you—"

"But I am," Roddy said. "You made it so easy for me, or anyone else. Too easy." Roddy smiled at her. The others were starting to look at him now. "You didn't lock your code down, Maj. You allowed access to it through the system using only one level of security. One password."

She stared at him. "You mean *you—How did you find it out?*"

"Come *on,* Maj," Roddy said. "Your grandparents' birthdays, your mother's and father's birthdays, and your brother's and sister's are matters of public record. So's yours, but at least you didn't make yourself look like a complete turnip by using *that.*"

"*Wait* a minute," Fergal said. "You sabotaged somebody's sim *again?*"

Roddy ignored him. Maj, meanwhile, could find nothing whatever to say.

"You didn't limit hours of access to your playroom either," Roddy continued. "And most to the point, you didn't take the simple precaution of running your code through a file-compare utility before you ran it yourself today. If you had, you would have seen everything I did. I think." He grinned again. "I wasn't as careless as you were. I didn't leave any obvious clues to what I was doing. The subroutines I added were scattered all through your code, not grouped, and the triggering sequences were encrypted. You shouldn't have too much trouble rooting them out. It won't take you more than a month or so, since I seeded the same routines through your backups as well, and you'll have to root those out too, to restore to your original format. Never hurts to be thorough.''

"Roddy," Chin said, rather slowly. "You pulled a stunt like this once before. Bob's Blackbird, wasn't it? You swore up and down you were never going to do it again."

Roddy actually shrugged. "You people just don't know how to take correction," he said. "I try to shake up your complacency a little, I try to show you that you're not covering your tails properly, try to make you function a little more professionally, and you go suborbital on me." He was actually smiling at them. "Can't you see that I'm trying to do you a favor? Someday when you get out in the *real* virtual world, you'll thank me."

"I wouldn't bet on it," Maj said. "I wouldn't thank you for the last glass of water in a desert, you—"

"Thought so. You can't take it either. And I thought you had such potential. My mistake . . . never mind. But Maj," Roddy said, ever so kindly, "maybe after this you better stick to the accordion."

She stared at him, absolutely transfixed with anger. Roddy disappeared from the playroom.

Maj looked around at all the others. Looking bemused, Bob said, "I didn't know you played the accordion."

"It is," Maj said, "almost the only instrument I *don't* play. I refuse to become the polka queen of Alexandria, Virginia. But that fracking little . . . Do you believe this! Do you *believe* this crap!"

She was almost stifled with her own rage. A couple of the others, never having seen Maj so angry before—never having seen her angry at all—hung back a little, plainly nonplussed and not knowing where to look.

"Since it wasn't your original simulation that caused this problem," Fergal said, "obviously none of us are going to try to make this run stick. Sorry, Mads."

There were other murmurs of "sorry" from around the group, but not from Alain. He stood stony-faced.

"And what about Roddy then?" Chin said. "Are we going to let him just waltz off after pulling a stunt like this *again*?"

Maj was appallingly grateful that she hadn't had to say it herself.

Sander was shaking his head now. "I don't know," he said in the slow way he had when he was feeling out of his depth, "but maybe he's right somehow. Maybe Maj should have been a little more careful." He turned to her. "I mean, come on, your grandmother's *birthday*? That's one of the first passwords a really malicious hacker would have come up with, if he knew anything about you at all. Maybe Roddy really was doing you a favor."

Maj looked at Sander's reasonable, broad face under that shock of blond hair and could do nothing but shake her head. "I can't *believe* you'd buy into that line of reasoning. In the real world, don't you think I would have chosen a password that no one could find?"

"But this is practice for the real world," Kelly said.

"Yes, well, but it's *practice*! And we've all agreed on that! Look, this is supposed to be a *safe* place to do our simming. We're supposed to be hard on each other's work, yeah, but we're not supposed to destroy it!"

"And now we have the same thing that he did to me before," Bob said. "The same approach. 'For your own good.' 'Can't you take a joke?' The same kind of thing they say to you on the playground when they push you off the teeter-totter. The only thing he forgot to call Maj was a crybaby. I'm surprised he missed it."

Alain snickered a little and turned away. "Well, that cuts close to the heart of it, doesn't it, Bob? You're still overreacting to what happened to *you*. And now Maj's doing it too. The problem here, Mads, is that he got you fair and square . . . and you're just a bad loser. You can't produce the goods, and when something bad happens as a result, you can't take it."

Maj turned on him so abruptly that even Alain took a step backwards, despite the virtuality of the situation. "I wouldn't indulge in in-depth analysis of the situation if I were you," she said softly, "because you're not exactly part of the solution. As if Roddy isn't bad enough by himself. You're always letting everybody know how brilliant he is. So he's brilliant! Good for him, and I hope it makes him rich and famous! But *you* make him worse. Don't think I don't hear your snide little asides to him every now and then. 'Go on, Roddy, you

can do it, you show him.' And he did. That's where he got
the bright idea to screw around with Bob's Blackbird in the
first place. And now this, after your remarks to Roddy last
week about 'seeing if she can produce the result in a compet-
itive environment.' Oh, I heard it, all right. So did some of
the others. Doesn't it seem to some of you that there might
just be a connection?''

" 'Just practice,' " Bob said. " 'Just a joke.' Some joke.''

Chin shook her head. "It was a little funny once.''

"To you maybe,'' Bob said. "Not to me.''

"Well, it was.'' Chin squirmed a little, but that was her
style, to tell the truth and not back down, no matter how uncomfortable it might make her, or the others around her. "The
second time you hear a joke, though, it's not so funny anymore. This sure wasn't. What about the third time? Which of
us is it going to be? And the fourth?''

Some heads were shaken.

"What do we do?'' Mairead said.

"Send him to Coventry,'' said Chin.

Coventry, heck, send him to jail! was Maj's first thought in
response to this. *What he did wasn't legal!* But at the same
time, she wasn't sure she wanted to be responsible for putting
someone in jail, no matter how humane and reforming jails
were supposed to be these days.

*But if he does it to me this way, illegally, who will he do it
to next? Better stop him now before he does it again.*

She stepped on that idea hard. It was likely enough to be
good old-fashioned paranoia at the moment. Still, such a
tempting image: to see the cop cars float down in front of his
house and . . .

No.

"Coventry?'' Fergal said, bemused. "Where's that?''

"Not a place,'' Chin said. "Well, yes, it is, but in this sense,
it's a state of mind. No communication with him. Isolation.''

"Not permanently, though?'' Fergal said.

Maj shook her head at that. "No. For all I know, he might
improve. But he's got to get the message that he can't just
trash people's sims to prove that he can do it.''

Fergal looked around at the group. All but Alain met his
gaze, and one by one they nodded. "Okay then,'' Fergal said.

"Nobody answers his virt-mails, nobody plays with any sims he's designed, no one has anything to do with him that isn't required by our business or 'real' lives. And as little of that as possible. I'll send him a mail and tell him what's happened."

"You have to set a time," Alain said, his voice very flat. "Some time when the sentence expires."

"No, we don't," Fergal said, looking around at the others again. "Why should we? He's on probation until we all decide otherwise. He doesn't like it, that's just tough." He looked at Maj. "Does that sound fair to you?"

She went hot again—embarrassment, and some other feeling that she couldn't then identify. "You shouldn't be trying to satisfy *me*. I'll recover."

"You will," Chin said, "but who knows how long it'll take you to debug your code? Roddy's good."

There was no arguing that, and it had been on Maj's mind.

"When she gets her code debugged then," Sander said.

Fergal nodded slowly. "Okay. Meanwhile—let's call it quits for tonight."

The group said its good-byes and vanished, one by one. Alain was one of the first to go, and the look he threw at Maj made her uncomfortable: as if *she* was somehow to blame for what Roddy had done. *I refuse to feel guilty about it,* she thought, and looked around her one last time at the high-desert morning, the mockingbird still singing scrambled excerpts from The Top Ten Songbird Songs of the Southwest, and the pillar of smoke still streaming up into the hard blue day, staining the pristine sky. "*Ho-yo-to-ho*, babydoll," she said softly, and spoke the password that would break her out of her playroom and back into reality.

The virtual world dissolved, and slowly the big family room asserted itself—the bookcases and the furniture all gloomy now, with only one light left on, over in the nearest corner of the room by the computer "boxes," the lamp her father had come to stand under when he spoke to her. There was no sign of him, not that she had particularly expected any. He was scheduled to be at some kind of faculty dinner tonight, something associated with the Georgetown University alumni association, what her dad referred to with rueful humor as "one of those ugly duties."

Maj got up out of the chair, stretching, and groaned a little. Her muscles were sore, despite the isometrics that the system applied to keep them working during what otherwise would have been long periods of immobility. *Probably somatic,* she thought. *I'm sore, all right. Sore at Roddy...*

She sighed. *Oh, frack, I forgot to get the gingerbread recipe.*

Maj didn't feel very much like going virtual again, but she had promised. She sat back down, lined her implant up with the computer again, and felt the little shock of the neural connection linking with the machine. Then she got up out of the chair—or seemed to—and walked through the door that appeared before her.

On the far side of it was woodland, the visual and tactile expression of her mother's virtual storage area. It was a sequoia forest, the great, tall silent boles of the trees spearing up on all sides, the pine needles deadening any sound from underfoot. Green sunlight came down through green shade, and the very faint piping sounds of birds could be heard at a distance, like single choristers practicing in some green cathedral.

Maj knew her way around here quite well. There were faint paths through the pine needles, some of them better trodden than others. She followed one of the ones that had seen more use than the rest lately, and made a turning around one of the larger trees.

In a clearing not far away was a gingerbread house, a chalet of the Swiss or Austrian type. Its roof was snowed over with sugar icing, and marzipan stones held the unseen mint-wafer roof tiles down here and there. Barley-sugar icicles hung down from the corners of the roof. The windows were candy-cane Gothic arches glazed with stained-sugar "glass" showing various scenes from Mother Goose, and the door appeared to be a slab of chocolate with licorice "wrought iron" binding, hinges, and door handles. Under the low eaves of the house on one side was a carefully cut and stacked pile of chocolate-coated graham-cracker firewood.

Maj looked at this apparition and sighed. *Anybody else,*

Maj thought, *would have just attached an icon to the recipe so that I could find it and pick it up to bring home. My* mother, *though . . .*

Her mother was a designer of other people's computer systems, and she was very good at it—but her sense of humor sometimes broke out in strange ways, and her definition of "object-oriented programming" was not one that many other people would have recognized. Maj, though, had seen it before. The woods in her mother's workspace were littered with not just symbols for objects, but the objects themselves: not small things symbolizing large ones, but large ones visualizing the small. It was a good thing that such a virtual space could be nearly limitless. It could get crowded. Its size aside, though, her mother's virtual space sometimes reminded her of a theme park.

Maj made a wry face and went over to the front of the house. She studied it for a moment, then reached out to one of the window shutters, a delicately made confection of pressed marzipan trying to look like painted wooden slats, and broke off a chunk of it. Her mother's "macro-icons" were all holographic in nature: A piece of one would reproduce the entire structure when reconstituted.

Abruptly the licorice door handle turned, and the chocolate door flow open. A little white-haired old lady, with a wrinkled but friendly face, wearing a long garnet-colored skirt, white shirt, and embroidered black vest, peered out at Maj . "Nibble, nibble, little mouse," said the old lady. "Who's that nibbling at my house?"

Maj gave her a look. "Buzz off, Grandma," she said, "or I'll show you how to check if your oven's preheated."

The witch made an annoyed face. "Kids these days," she said, and slammed the door.

Maj sighed. "You don't know the half of it," she said, and made her way back through the forest. Among the trees she found a galvanized garbage can labeled KITCHEN. Maj tossed the chunk of sugar into it, sighed, and headed wearily back down the pathway out into the real world. The task awaiting her there, if Roddy had done half the damage she was afraid he might have, was formidable. And there was no time better than the present to begin the work of rebuilding. . . .

3

Two weeks later, Alain Thurston strode through a virtual landscape on the fringes of the Net, smiling to himself as he went. All around him the bleak, gray, treeless vista of plains and barren hills was whipped by the winds associated with a mighty storm building over the nearby mountains. Those mountains had an unfriendly look, spiky and brutal. The valleys between them were dark, except where iron-gray mist poured down them from the clouds clotting and massing above. It was the kind of landscape that suggested it had been produced by a writer of bad epic fantasy who was suffering from dyspepsia, or who had an excessive number of stereotypical Evil Characters who needed housing.

Alain knew what was inside those mountains, and grinned a little to himself as he hiked toward the scree-slope leading to the foot of the biggest one, the mountain that ended this particular chain. *This is going to be fun,* he thought. *Poor Roddy . . .*

Alain thought of himself as one of those people for whom the Net had been made. He spent as little time nonvirtual every day as he could. School—well, there was little enough he could do about high school. He was stuck with it for another year and a half yet. Of course, the possibility of college was looming on the horizon like a big black cloud . . . but Alain was already working on his folks in that regard. They had proven deaf to his protests that there was more to life than a college degree. All his mother could go on about was the value of further education, yadda-yadda-yadda, until it nearly made him crazy. Alain had therefore been carefully putting himself out of the running by letting his grades quietly go to hell.

He wasn't too concerned about this. Alain knew he was smart—and unfortunately, so did Alain's guidance counselor. There was no way he could make the man shut up and stop his complaining, nor would there be any way to do this short of Alain getting out of school and free of Mr. MacIlwain at last. Alain was certainly too smart to spend another four years hammering his head against yet another batch of dimwit teachers when the big world of business and freedom and money was out there right now.

When Alain eventually felt like doing something, getting a job or whatever, he knew he'd have no trouble doing it. He was already pretty good at simming, for example, and there were plenty of companies hiring. Alain could get himself a job anytime he wanted one. Meanwhile, there was enough money to get by on—his dad still gave him an allowance, along with weekly or sometimes daily lectures intended to get Alain to straighten up and fly right.

By this time next year the last GSAT scores would be in, and they would make it plain that Alain was not going to be accepted by any college of sufficient standing for Alain's father to be willing to admit that his son was going there. That would be the end of *that* problem. Then (or soon after then) Alain would move out and find a job, and become successful and (after not too long) wealthy, and everything would be fine.

Maybe he would even look into joining Net Force. He had a contact there, the beautiful Ms. Rachel Halloran, who would smooth his way, and the thought of being affiliated with the most powerful organization in the virtual world had its attractions. But despite the power and prestige that came with being accepted into Net Force, he wasn't sure it was for him. He wasn't sure about the idea of being tied down into a situation where he would have any bosses but himself, at least not until he'd made it plain that he could be his own boss just as easily.

He was going to kick butt out there in the real world, he just knew it. He could hardly wait to show his folks how wrong they were about him. But he had to get through high school before he was free to take off. So there was plenty of time to work all that out.

Meanwhile, he was coasting. He showed up at school every day, sat in the assigned seat in each assigned room, and did as much as he felt like of the assigned work, real or virtual—usually not very much. This was what Alain and a couple of his cronies referred to as the Minimum Assured Destruction plan: meaning that, by cooperating this much but no more with the school Establishment, they would destroy no more than the minimum number of their brain cells, which were much more profitably engaged in things like, well, like simming.

Alain had stumbled onto the Group of Seven nearly a year before, while casually wandering through the open virtual discussion groups that were a fixture of almost every part of the Net, both public and private. At that point, the Group was still simming in a public group-area that went by the old protocol-hierarchy name *virt.alt.gaming.simulations*—but they were not going to be there for long. The discussion groups in the *virt.alt* hierarchy were not moderated, so besides involving a fair number of people genuinely interested in discussing the topic of high-quality virtual simulation, they also involved a much larger group, sometimes hundreds of thousands of people, who just sat around watching and listening to everything you said and did, but who contributed nothing. And additionally, like every other public virt-group, *virt.alt.gaming.simulations* featured a fair number of fruitcakes, nutcases, blown diodes, cracked solids, and other nuisance types who lived merely to use up disk space, bother or insult people, and keep anything really worthwhile from happening.

Alain was not one to mind the occasional well-honed insult every now and then, especially when someone had been dumb enough to leave themselves open for it—but people who had nothing *but* weak-witted flames and bad language to contribute were, he reckoned, a waste of his valuable time. Before he'd joined the Group of Seven, the people who'd formed the Group had thought the same. They had agreed to "go private," each paying a monthly subscription fee to create and maintain a small restricted simming space where they could talk and construct their projects without half the population of the planet looking on and interrupting the smooth flow of business.

These first seven had formed the Group of the same name. Alain had known one of them—Fergal—and had wangled an invitation into the Group from him. The others had looked at Alain's "submission" sim, a simulation of that ancient and venerable steam engine the "Rocket," and had found it good—as damn well they should have—and had admitted him to the Group.

Alain stopped at the foot of the mountain at the end of the chain, puffing a little, and looked up at the sheer, forbidding cliffs that reared up above his head. He had enjoyed himself moderately since he joined the Group of Seven, becoming its eighth. He had learned a few things, and had taught the rest of them a lot. All right, so *they* never admitted it. They were not quite as smart a bunch as they thought, which tended to make them all a little sensitive about praising other people's work, and when they messed up, as poor, stupid Maj had today, they tended to overreact. No matter. They kept Alain in practice for the job he was certain to land as soon as he decided to strike out into the big world and show his dad that he didn't know everything there was to know about the job market.

Meanwhile, there were minor entertainments among the personalities in the group. Fergal was still friendly enough, though sometimes Alain caught Fergal looking at him in a way he didn't quite understand. Something in his gaze seemed not entirely approving. Well, who needed his approval anyway? *But Roddy, though,* Alain thought. Roddy was another story entirely. Alain grinned again, and started up the scree-slope that led up into the darkest of the valleys under the mountain.

He and Roddy had met only in the virtual realm, as so many people did these days when genuine travel was sometimes appallingly expensive compared to "telepresence." It was during some discussion in a gaming group that had turned into a shouting match . . . as was all too likely when Roddy was involved. Alain had walked into the virtual landscape in question—in this case, it had been a rocky slope at the bottom of which the battle of Thermopylae was taking place—to find nine tenths of the people involved in the simulation yelling at

Roddy, under whose auspices the Spartans had somehow been ambushed before they were properly emplaced. Thermopylae went on resolving itself in the valley below, the groans and cries of the dying being drowned out by the enraged bellows of the gamers, and of Roddy, who couldn't make them understand that he had just been doing them a favor.

The scene was so bizarre that when the other gamers stormed off and left Roddy to himself among the corpses, Alain stayed and started to talk to him . . . and after about five minutes of conversation realized that here was one of those people around whom life would never be dull. Granted, Roddy *looked* dull enough: big but pudgy for seventeen, with a blobby, unfinished look to him, wearing an unprepossessing face in which nothing but his eyes seemed alive.

Until Roddy smiled—and then that smile would make you either take a step back, or just stare in astonishment at the curl of pure, unconscious, joyous malice in it, like that of a baby in a high chair who's just discovered the lovely noise a dish makes when he drops it on the floor and breaks it. Soon the baby learns to do this "accidentally," of course, and Roddy had a smile of that kind too, to suit occasions when he had premeditated some particular piece of work that would make him look good and someone else look bad. But the measure of his genius was that he could produce such results *without* even premeditating them. Alain found this hilarious, and he decided to keep Roddy around.

It had been a smart move, for Roddy was not stupid, not in the slightest. He certainly was lacking in what an earlier generation would have called "social graces." No one would hang out with him long enough for him to develop any. Alain himself had been annoyed by Roddy more than once, but kept him around anyway because . . . well, because you never knew. He might be useful. That gift Roddy had for looking as if he had planned some dire nasty act even when it had been accidental, a quirk of circumstance . . . something like that, Alain reasoned, could come in useful someday if *he* was planning something nasty, and needed someone to take the fall.

Alain reached the top of the scree-slope and paused. Here the stairs began, a wide stairway of granite, zigzagging up the side of the mountain along what had once been the wall of a glacial cirque. Getting his breath back, he started to climb again, thinking about which direction to turn Roddy in now.

It was so easy, after all, to manipulate Roddy in one direction or another. He never caught on until it was too late. He would yell and carry on about it for a while, but that never lasted long—and after that, with Alain anyway, Roddy would actually be contrite about it. He knew he wasn't much good at having friends. He was afraid to lose the one who had stuck by him for this long. Their frendship was something of a record for Roddy, Alain suspected.

He paused at the first switchback of the stairs, looking down the way he had come, to the scree-slope and the flat, unhappy landscape all around him. Maj had been right, in her small way. Alain had suggested that Roddy take her down a peg or so, and Roddy had seen to it . . . big time. Perhaps rather bigger time than Alain would have—his methods tended to be subtler—but it was still fun to see the stuck-up little broad at a loss. Oh, the sim itself had been nice enough in its way, but she should have known to stick to something simpler until she understood what she was doing. Alain had been ready to bet she would keep a slightly lower profile in the Group for a while, while he (and Roddy) turned their attention to one of the others who needed one kind of object lesson or another.

Yet now, Alain thought, at the second switchback—only one more to go, and he could see the hulking shapes of the guards standing outside the great doors above as he started walking again—*now things have gone a little differently than I had expected.* This "shunning" thing, this "sending someone to Coventry." If Alain wanted to stay in the Group, he was going to have to cooperate. Even by this virtual visit, he was breaking the rules . . . and if the others found out . . .

But they won't find out. The important thing is to make sure that things keep going the way I want them to. They can impose this little "sentence" on Roddy until Maj gets her code sorted out again. It won't take her more than a month or so. Maybe I'll even help. Alain had to smile at the thought. It would be easy enough to get Roddy to tell him where he had built his various levels of sabotage into Maj's code. Then he could go to Maj and "help" her. She'd be grateful to him, in her too-noble way. Someone else who could be useful to him, sometime, somewhere down the road . . .

He finally came out on the slate-flagged terrace in front of the door, and went up to the guards, who had moved forward to block his path. They were large ugly monsters in tattered rusty mail: bipedal, with two arms and a head at the top, but that was about all you could say in their favor. Their skin was gray, their hair was gray, their teeth were gray (where they weren't brown—either these things drank too much tea, or they had other habits about which Alain refused to speculate). They had tusks, like boars, and little piggy eyes that looked out from under beetly brows on which perched, somewhat precariously, beat-up late-Norman helmets. They had sharp, stained spears, on which they leaned, and they looked at Alain with unfriendly expressions, expressions suggesting that he would be best employed as cold cuts.

Alain had seen this look before. It was a variant of one Roddy sometimes wore in unguarded moments, and Alain sometimes wondered whether it appeared on the faces of these servitors entirely as a conscious irony. "The boss is expecting me," Alain said. "Didn't anybody ever teach you not to stare? Get outta my way."

The guards looked at Alain slowly, then even more slowly moved back from where they had come to stand in the doorway, as if the command from their brains was making its way down to the muscles not by bioelectricity but by hand messenger. Alain brushed past them, holding his breath. It did not do to breathe too deeply around most of Roddy's servants.

Alain stepped into the darkness and paused for a moment to let his eyes get used to the changed light inside. Specifically, there was no light inside that did not come from torches fixed to the walls, and the walls, by and large, were far away. The whole inside of the mountain was hollowed out.

He started walking across the crevassed, stone-floored space. Roddy's virtual workspace was the Hall of the Mountain King—or at least if the composer Grieg had been dropped into the middle of it, he would have recognized it as such. Gray, stark, stony walls rose up on all sides, and everywhere on the huge, stalagmited floor the myriad brothers of the guards at the door—they might have passed for genetically engineered orcs—scurried about doing their master's bidding. Some of them had more legs than they needed. Some, rather pointedly, had less, as if someone had been pulling limbs off them the way a bored and nasty child might pull the wings off flies. It was not as if Alain particularly subscribed to the Be Kind to Your Creation ethic that some on-line creators touted so noisily, but he didn't believe in letting the cruelty be quite so overt. It was unsubtle. He avoided meeting the eyes of the trolls and orcs who were pulling themselves along the floor by just their clawy hands, and kept on walking.

Alain walked up toward the far end of the hall, where a fire burned in a big open pit, and behind it, in a huge stone throne carved rudely out of a particularly massive stalagmite, sat Roddy. He was watching Alain—he never took his eyes off him all the while Alain walked the quarter mile or so to the throne.

Alain was used to this staring trick. As he got closer, though, something else put him slightly on his guard. Roddy was doing something with his hands, fiddling with something between them, manipulating something that spilled down into his lap and down onto the floor beside the throne, where it made a tangled bright pile like a skein of unwound yarn set on fire.

As Alain got to within twenty feet or so of the throne, he saw what Roddy was working with in more detail. It appeared to be a giant strand of DNA, and he was unraveling it at one end, the nucleic acid bonds hanging off the two main spiraling strands like rungs of a ladder come loose from the ladder's sides.

Alain wondered. Symbologies varied wildly in the virtual world—that being one of the most delightful things about it—but when you were working with so well-known a symbol as DNA, there was little point in "seeing" it as anything else. *What's he up to now?* Alain thought. There was never any telling with Roddy, except that it tended to be brilliant.

"Took you long enough to get here," Roddy said, breaking that fixed gaze at Alain to glance down at the "knitting" again.

"I came as soon as I could. Schoolwork—"

"Give me a break," Roddy said. "You promised *them* you wouldn't come."

"Strictly political," Alain said. "No way they could find out whether I came or not."

"Then why wait so long?" Roddy said, looking up again.

Alain held his face straight, so as not to let out any hint of his thought: that there was no harm in letting the tension rise a little at this end of things. Keeping Roddy a little nervous about Alain's loyalties struck Alain as smart.

But Roddy didn't look nervous . . . in fact, rather the opposite. His posture was leisurely. He had his feet propped up on a stone "hassock" as he manipulated the stranded construct with which he was working, and he glanced down at it, casually, as if debating whether to knit one or purl two.

"Look, I got busy. Some of us have lives outside this, you know." He glanced around him at the stone and the hurrying orcs.

"Waste of time," Roddy said, finished with one part of the "knitting," and started to run it through his hands a little more quickly, like cabling, as if he was looking for one specific piece. "Nothing out there as interesting as in here. 'Lives'—they're overrated."

This was a theme Alain had heard Roddy elaborate before . . . though not one he particularly wanted to hear him get started on now. Roddy could become practically unhinged if he kept going on about it long enough. Alain had no idea what Roddy's home life was like, and he didn't want to know. "Maybe," Alain said. "Whatcha working on?"

"A piece of my next playroom," Roddy said.

"Oh? What's it going to be?"

"I'm not going to be discussing that just yet," Roddy said. "I'll be ready to have people start looking at it at the end of the week, though."

"You mean the Group?"

"I had thought of inviting them," Roddy said, "among others."

Alain blinked at that. "They won't come."

"Oh, yes, they will."

"Uh, Rod, I don't know if you're clear about how sparked off they all are. If you hadn't—"

"But I did," Roddy said, pausing to examine a specific portion of the DNA molecule, and then going back to running it quickly through his hands again. "Not that they had the brains to understand what I was trying to do to them. For them. And that little slitch Maj," Roddy said, "this whole thing is *her* fault."

"Yeah, it—what?" Alain looked at Roddy in slight bemusement. "How do you mean?"

"She was supposed to just fold up and go away," Roddy muttered. "Not stand up, not fight. She doesn't have any fight in her."

"I wouldn't say *that.* . . . "

Roddy looked up again, eyes flashing. "She didn't! She didn't until the Group started encouraging her! Now look what she's done to me! She would never have opened her mouth if you hadn't—" Roddy stopped suddenly.

"You showed her real good," Alain said as soothingly as he could. "You should have seen her virt-mails."

"Send me copies," Roddy said.

"Uh, I erased them," Alain said hurriedly, since in fact he had seen no virt-mails from Madeline at all.

"I was expecting," Roddy said, looking down at his "knitting" again, "that they would have rethought their actions after a day or two. Would have extended their mercy to the poor 'misunderstood' member of the Group. But they didn't." Roddy's glance snapped up to Alain again, that abrupt sharp look in his eyes. "I thought you would have talked them into it."

"I tried to stand up for you, Rod. They weren't listening."

"You must not have stood up very hard. . . ." The tone was suddenly silky. Roddy looked down at his DNA again, passing it through his hands more slowly now.

Alain shook his head. "Roddy, they were *all* out after you. I don't want to be kicked out of the Group, and they were *that* far away from suggesting it, some of them!"

"Well, I think it's getting to be time to start another group," Roddy said, his voice angry again. "One where people are willing to listen to what I have to say . . . instead of me having to knuckle under to everybody else's ideas of 'nice behavior.' I've had about enough of it. Well, this new playroom will contain the kernel for another kind of group . . . one that everyone who sims is going to want to join. They'll all see, later in the week. *You'll* see too . . . assuming you have the time to stop by.''

Alain looked at him in slight unease. This kind of determination was a little strange in Roddy . . . and his usual attempts to keep Alain friendly toward him seemed not to be materializing. *What brought this on?* Alain thought—and wondered again, if only very briefly, about what might be going on with Roddy at home.

''Here,'' Roddy said abruptly, ''catch.'' He threw Alain a torn-off bit of the DNA he had been fiddling with.

Caught off guard, Alain caught the strand of double helix before he was entirely aware of what he was doing. He stared at it, turned it over in his hands. It was peculiarly beautiful. It shone, and the light clung about his hands. ''Nice,'' he said, and tossed it back.

Roddy gave him a somber look as he grabbed the strand. ''Yeah,'' he said, ''it is.'' He glanced down at the pile of similar strands that lay partially supported by the side of the throne. ''Well. I've got to get back to work on the new playroom.''

''Rod, they *won't* go to it,'' Alain said. ''Even I shouldn't go to it. Not at first,'' he added somewhat hurriedly . . . and he wasn't sure why. ''Though once Madeline gets her code debugged, things will be easier.'' He shook his head, and grinned in brief and momentarily sincere admiration. ''That was some job you did on her. Wouldn't surprise me if she needed some help sorting it out.'' He let the grin go a little wider. ''Now, if someone were to give her a few hints . . . not that it would be as if they actually *knew* where the problems were, you understand . . .''

''Oh, I don't know,'' Roddy said. ''I think she should be left to work this out for herself, don't you? A growth experience. It'll be good for her.''

He gave Alain another look that was peculiarly somber, then glanced down at his ''knitting'' one more time. ''As for the playroom,'' Roddy said very offhandedly, ''what she made me do to her the other day won't matter, to her or to the rest of the Group, not as far as the playroom's concerned. They'll all come eventually. They won't be able to resist. I know them better than they think I do . . . and there's one thing they've got that'll make them come.''

Alain looked at him uncomprehendingly, wondering what was going on with Roddy. Something a lot different than usual . . . more studied somehow. Alain was going to have to get a handle on it fast, before Roddy started becoming unmanageable. Unmanageable by Alain anyway. "Like what?'' Alain asked.

"Like what made you come today,'' Roddy said.

Does he mean loyalty? Alain thought. *What a laugh.*

"They'll be along,'' Roddy said. "And wait'll you see what they find waiting for them. They'll all be blown away. Even you will . . .''

"Well,'' Alain said, "let's see what you come up with first. I'm not that easy to blow away.''

Roddy smiled. Alain shuddered, for it was not Roddy's usual smile. It was a look of pure pleasure without the malice . . . and that sudden lack confused Alain badly.

"I think you'll be impressed,'' Roddy said.

"Yeah, well, we'll see,'' Alain said. "Look, just make sure none of the others know we've been talking.''

"It'll never occur to them, I'm sure,'' Roddy said. "You go ahead. I'll drop you a virt-mail when things are ready. Shouldn't take more than a few days. I'm a good ways along.''

"Okay,'' Alain said. "You need anything for this piece of work that I can dig up for you? Save you a little time while you're concentrating?''

"Oh, no,'' Roddy said almost sweetly. "I have everything I need, believe me. But thanks for asking.''

"Right,'' Alain said. "See you then.''

"Whenever,'' said Roddy in that casual voice, the voice that sounded like he had no worries, none at all. Alain waved a hand casually and headed off down the long expanse of the Hall of the Mountain King. Orcs scurried to get away from him as he came. Alain ignored them, for he was listening for the sound of laughter, for Roddy's usual soft chuckle, behind his back.

He didn't hear it. Odd . . . for Roddy liked to play the theatrical villain in here usually: flames leaping from the crevasses' that split the floor here and there, cowed servitors scuttling, shadows and darkness. . . .

Alain paused and looked over his shoulder. Roddy just sat there in the throne with his feet up, oblivious, his head bowed again over his work, "knitting."

Confused by this new behavior from Roddy, Alain turned and walked on out again, heading for the guards at the doors. *This new playroom . . . if he really does well with it . . . and suddenly gets the idea that he doesn't need me for anything anymore . . .*

Maybe this is an idea it would be good to interfere with. Alain smiled to himself. *I need to look into how to reassert the status quo . . . and teach him that there are things he needs me around for . . . that he can't just fast-mouth me the way he does everybody else. Now, if something were to go wrong with this new playroom of his, for example . . . or people turned out not to think it was as hot as Roddy thinks they should find it . . .*

He smiled again. He would get to work on this as soon as he could.

At the door, the guards moved aside as Alain walked between them, already starting to think how to turn this situation to his best advantage. . . .

But he did not see the smirk they exchanged behind him as Alain vanished back into the real world.

4

Saturday morning a week and a half later dawned sunny over Alexandria, Virginia: a briefly cool morning before what promised to be a relentlessly hot and sticky day. The cicadas were already doing some stop-and-start shrilling by eight in the morning. It was their racket that woke Maj up so early on what would normally have been a day when she would have relished sleeping late.

Resigned, for she was one of those people who couldn't get back to sleep once they woke up in the morning, Maj got up and showered and dressed, and made her way through the rambling house toward the kitchen. It was a bit of a walk. The place had been built in the early 1950s, and its numerous owners since then had added many bits and pieces to it over time: a carport here, an extension bedroom there, a dormer up here—all the parts being of varying quality, and some now in much better repair than others. As a result, her family had a house that was a bit of an architectural surd (in her mother's affectionately scornful phrase), and seemed at times to be mostly held together with duct tape in places where the joints between wings and additions were beginning to suffer from the ravages of time.

In the kitchen she got herself a cup of Japanese roasted-rice tea and considered the day before her. She might go riding later, if it didn't get too hot. She was not feeling particularly musical today. Friday night had involved a long and grueling pre-recital session with the youth chamber group in which she played viola, and she didn't want to hear anyone so much as whistle at the moment—this being her usual reaction to over-exposure to one particular piece. They had gone over one part of Tartini's *Violin Concerto in E minor* last night until she felt like her eyes were going to bleed. *No,* Maj thought, *just lovely peace and quiet today.* Which left her with the unavoidable job that had been piling up all week: her virt-mail.

She sat down at the kitchen table and had a long drink of the tea first. Some of the mail Maj had been ignoring harder than usual . . . especially stuff from the other members of the Group of Seven.

It was as much from embarrassment as anything else. Even though she knew she really had no reason to be embarrassed about the way her sim had crashed, considering what Roddy had done to it, it was hard to avoid the feeling. She was used to at least seeming more competent than she had . . . and Roddy's gibe about the password, cruel though it might have been, was true. She'd learned *that* lesson anyway, but it didn't keep her from feeling heartsore when she went into her play-room.

Which she was going to have to do again this morning. She had put it off all week, using schoolwork as the excuse. It was a lousy excuse, and had fooled no one, not in her family at least. Maj had found herself doing things she would never have normally done: the dishes (by hand, causing her father to feel her forehead); the year's last school project, which wasn't due for two months yet (Maj normally had a healthy ability to procrastinate until almost the moment before she would absolutely have to start something). She had even ven-tured into her mother's workroom at the back of the house, that den of piled-up fabric cuttings and plywood and styro-foam and endless other remnants and artifacts of craft projects past and future, and had offered to help her mom while she was engaged in the more difficult parts of gingerbread-house construction (getting the walls glued in place with the sugar-and-egg-white icing was usually the worst part). Her mother had looked at her with an expression halfway between pity and suspicion, then had shooed her out with the cryptic pro-nouncement ''You'd better just get back on the horse.''

Well, it wasn't that *cryptic,* Maj thought. She knew that much from her own riding. If you got thrown, you got back on . . . not only because otherwise you might lose your nerve. Much more important was the fact that if you didn't get right back on, the horse's opinion of you would plummet. Horses might be stupid about some things, but they were also extremely opinionated . . . and once you showed them cowardice, they would never respect you again.

So she would have to "get back on" and get busy with her simming again . . . but not right this minute. Maj put the teacup down with a sigh, then got up and sat in the extra implant chair at the end of the table. It was (her father said) an extravagance, but (her mother insisted) a useful one, and Maj was inclined to agree, since with it there she could sit in the kitchen and eat buttered toast (genuine) while taking care of her mail (virtual).

She got herself set up within a few seconds, letting the "living room" of her personal space coexist with the kitchen for the moment. This meant that the big slightly fake antique space—her father's brainchild, with its matte-black granite counters and massive cooking fireplace and slate-flagged floor, and the big rough-scrubbed table with the antique drying rack above it, hung with bunches of herbs—now appeared to Maj to butt "up against" Maj's own virtual environment, which ran to brushed stainless-steel furniture and cabinets, stark white walls, a high cathedral ceiling, and above it, visible through the skylight of the retractable roof, the hard blue sky of a brilliant winter day in the Mediterranean, seen from one of the Peloponnesian Islands.

The two environments looked odd juxtaposed this way. For amusement's sake, Maj had seen to it that the places where they joined in her VR were apparently held together with duct tape. Her father had passed through in the virtual world and had seen the duct tape that ran rampant in her space a few months back—then had exited suddenly, without comment, though his shoulders had been shaking as if he was trying to keep from cracking up.

Maj made herself one more cup of tea, then sat back down at the kitchen table and started taking care of the piled-up mail, one piece at a time. All around her in the air floated the three-dimensional icons, each of which denoted a separate piece of mail. The ones she had already dealt with were off on her left, and the unhandled ones floated to her right. Some of the left-hand ones had originally had the cube- or pyramid-shapes given to them by various commercial or proprietary virt-mail programs, but now they looked like crumpled-up pieces of paper ready to be thrown into a trash can. Maj was never hasty about throwing away even the junk mail. She was always ready to have second thoughts about things . . . though in the case of this particular batch of mail, it seemed unlikely.

She glanced over at a large group of crumpled-up messages that all had one thing in common: Roddy L'Officier's virt-mail address.

She had been "ignoring" his virt-mails since the crashing of her sim—not that she found it difficult to ignore mails that came in with headers like ATTENTION: BACKSTABBING SLITCH. On one level, the number of infuriated responses from him was simply satisfying—one reason Maj had let them keep coming, rather than just telling the system to refuse them outright. But on another level, the messages fed her annoyance at Roddy, for Maj had little time for people whose first response, on being handed an annoyance by life, was to descend into bad language.

Not that she was at all prudish about it—she could swear with the best of them—but she couldn't forget her dad's reaction one day when she'd let fly with a few choice expletives in front of him. He had paused for a moment, halfway into the living room where a pile of papers were sitting awaiting grading, then walked by her, saying mildly, "But Maj, what will you have left to say when you hit your thumb with a hammer?"

Maj made a wry face. After getting a clearer sense of the mess Roddy had made of her code, she had been more than willing to exhaust her bad-word options for a good long while. But it wouldn't have helped. Nothing was going to help her sim except about a month and a half of debugging. There was not a single routine or subroutine that Roddy had not gotten at, leaving snide little comments in "remarks" fields every-where through the program. She'd found them in every version of her program and all her backups as well. Roddy was unquestionably a talented programmer, but at the moment, Maj would have been most pleased to drop a rock on his head, and not a virtual one.

Meanwhile, the only thing she could do was throw away his mails . . . which she was doing with pleasure. She'd made the mistake of reading one or two of them in passing, thinking she would be adult enough to handle more of his insults. Well, maybe she was, if "handling" involved having to get up and stomp around the kitchen and make yet another cup of tea and drink it every time she read one. His nasty, supercilious, I-know-better-than-you-you-poor-brain-damage-case attitude was just so *infuriating*.

She breathed out, reached out into the air, and grabbed one more of the icons hovering over the right-hand side of the kitchen table. FROM: RODDY L'OFFICIER, said the truncated header information, which appeared glowing in the air as she took hold of the icon. TO: MADELINE GREEN. SUBJECT: YOUR PUSILLANIMOUS—

Maj grimaced, and clenched the icon in her fist. It turned into crumpled paper, and she chucked it over with all the rest of them . . . then sighed and reached out for another of the right-hand icons. TO: MADELINE GREEN. FROM: FRIEND5277536. SUBJECT: YOU MAY ALREADY BE A WINNER—

This time she smiled a little as she crumpled the icon up and threw it away. *At least it's* honest *junk mail,* she thought, and reached out for the next icon. There was this consolation too, that the rest of the Group of Seven were doing no better as regarded the contents of their mailboxes than she was. All of them were being snowed under by endless angry and abusive virt-mails from Roddy, which they were rejecting or otherwise refusing to respond to.

There had been some talk among the Group about the possibility of complaining to his service provider and seeing whether they could make him stop, but if Roddy's account got pulled, he would only get madder, and get another account somewhere else, and start the whole business all over again. If they genuinely hoped to rehabilitate him, even a little, it was better not to bother. They were all in favor of tossing the offending mail and letting Maj finish her debugging as fast as possible, so that the Group could cancel the "Coventry" ban without looking as if they had wimped out.

Maj picked up another icon, and then paused, hearing a sound. Her little sister, wearing footie pajamas and her usual early-morning disordered blond curls, came wandering in through the real side of the kitchen with a large picture book under her arm. She went over to the big side-by-side refrigerator, pulled the fridge-side door open, and stared in. And stared. And stared.

Maj sighed. "Muf, come on, shut the door."

"I'm just looking," Muffin said. Her real name was Adrienne, but about the middle of last year, on turning five, Maj's little sister had suddenly declared that she hated that name, and from now on would be known as Muffin. She had then steadfastly refused to answer to any other name, and after a while the family had accepted it . . . overtly. "We'll see if she still wants to be called Muffin when she gets to school and the other kids start exploring the name's teaseability," their mother had said. Right now, though, her little sister was oblivious to this prospect . . . and apparently also to Maj.

"Muffie . . ." Maj said. "Come on. All the cold's getting out."

Muffin continued to stare into the fridge.

"If you don't shut the door, everything in there will rot and go hairy," Maj said, "and stuff will come crawling out at night and hide under your bed. . . ."

"No, it won't," the Muffin said, but smiled a small eldritch smile and closed the refrigerator door, apparently charmed by this image. She came over to the table and reached up to set her book on it. "You're staring at nothing again."

"I'm doing my virt-mail, Muffles," Maj said.

"Okay. Maj, I saw a *dinosaur*!"

"Oh," Maj said, looking away from the crumpled icons again. "Which kind, honey?"

"An archipelagus." She pronounced the word with due care and a small space between each syllable.

"Is that a real one, Muf, or one you made up?" The way they kept changing dinosaur names from the ones Maj had learned when she was young, it was getting more difficult to tell whether the Muffin's etymology was genuine or mythological. Let alone to work out whether the things Muffin had "seen" were virtual or not. At age five, it was sometimes difficult to tell.

Maj had heard people arguing for a long while now about whether it was wise to let children under seven into the virtual world at all. Some people claimed that young children couldn't tell the difference between reality and fantasy below that age, and that too-early exposure to virtuality could corrupt a child's ability to tell reality from virtuality later. Other people said that the sooner you trained a child to tell the difference, the better they'd be able to survive in a world becoming increasingly virtual. Maj wasn't sure which side of the argument was right, but the one thing she felt fairly sure of was that the kids being argued over were, by and large, a lot smarter than either side gave them credit for.

"Of *course* it's real," her sister said, looking at Maj as if she had a board loose. "Everything's *real*." She pulled out the nearest kitchen chair, climbed up into it, sat down, and opened the book, that faint slight smile still twitching at the corners of her mouth.

Maj looked at that smile and wondered how many of her legs were being pulled, and how hard. "Thank you, Miss Muffaletta," she said, and went back to the consideration of her mail.

She chucked a few more crumpled examples of Roddy's alleged wit off to the left, along with several more unwanted ads, the kind that start with "If you have been sent this message in error, please inform us and accept our apologies" and "To be removed from our mailing list, please send your virtmail information to the following address." Both were sure ways to get much more electronic junk if you answered them and thereby confirmed that your virt-mail account was indeed active. There were also a couple of genuine messages from other people in the Group of Seven.

The one that made her chuckle right out loud was a note from Alain, offering to help her debug her code. Besides her uncertainty that Alain would be able to do any better at it than she was doing at the moment, Maj had some private questions about his motivations. He and Roddy were too cozy by half. It wouldn't surprise her if this was actually some kind of covert move on Roddy's part to see how she was doing at the debugging.

Paranoid, Maj thought. And immediately answered herself, *Well, even paranoiacs have real enemies.* . . . She sighed, not much liking the frame of mind that the last couple of weeks' events had left her in.

Someone knocked on the brushed stainless-steel door in the virtual workspace behind her. Maj turned her head, unconcerned. There were only a few people who her workspace had been instructed to allow in that far. "Come in."

The door opened, and a tall, dark-haired, broad-shouldered man in jeans and a fuzzy plaid shirt walked in, looking around him casually. *James Winters—!* Maj's eyebrows went straight up into her hairline. She put down her cup of tea in mid-sip, and swallowed hurriedly. "Mr. Winters," she said. "Hi, come on in."

"Don't get up," he said. "It's not a formal visit."

Maj wondered about that, even as she pulled out a chair for him. The public relations liaison for Net Force wouldn't normally come by on *in*formal visits . . . except, Maj thought, that *this* man would. The Net Force Explorers, of whom Maj was one, were one of his special interests. It was probably self-interest as much as altruism—any policing organization needs a valid recruitment mechanism, one which will attract and "bring on" new blood—but in Winters's case, Maj thought the involvement was more personal.

He gave the impression of being one of those people who genuinely remembers how it feels to be young—as opposed to someone who was merely hanging on to the very filtered and sanitized image of adolescence that was all that most adults allowed themselves. As a result, the kids with whom Winters worked would gladly put themselves out on the line for him. They knew he would return the favor.

"Just doing the rounds," Winters said as he sat down. "A quiet weekend for once . . . I thought I'd stop around and see the Irregulars on something besides business, if they weren't already otherwise occupied." Maj smiled slightly at that. Winters was a Sherlock Holmes fan, which many of the Net Force Explorers had started to become over time—mostly in self-defense, so that they could understand references to things like the Baker Street Irregulars and so on without looking like the terminally clueless.

Winters sat back and looked around him at the ultramodern interior of Maj's "Greek villa." He smiled slightly. "You got tired of the castle, I take it."

"Too drafty," Maj said. "Even with the stained glass in the windows."

Winters looked around at the various icons floating in the air. "I'm not interrupting anything important, am I?"

"Oh, no," Maj said. "Just the mail." She rolled her eyes at the crumpled icons. "Mostly junk."

Across the table, the Muffin looked up. "Maj, why'd you pull the chair out?"

"Mr. Winters came to visit," Maj said.

"Oh," the Muffin said. "Maj, is he your Invisible Friend?"

Maj flushed hot and laughed at the same time. The Muffin had recently discovered the advantages of having an Invisible Friend who wanted some more ice cream, or one more ride in the rowboat on the park lake—taking the heat for asking for such things off *her,* of course.

"No, Muf," Maj said, "he's real, but he's on the virtual side at the moment."

"Okay." The Muffin went back to her book.

"Heard you had a bad day recently," Winters said.

Maj rolled her eyes again. "News gets around fast," she said. "Where did you hear?"

"Mark Gridley. He sims apparently."

Maj nodded, filing that piece of information away. She had met Mark, the Net Force director's son, in connection with the Explorers, but couldn't really say she knew him well. He was a hotshot with anything virtual, in fact with anything computer-based—another of those natural talents, though a benevolent one, completely unlike Roddy. *A relief: Two Roddys in the world would be two too many,* Maj thought uncharitably but with pleasure. "Yeah, he would have heard," she said after a moment. "The word got out into the open newsgroups after a day or two."

"You okay?"

Maj grinned slightly. "Any crash you walk away from is a good one," she said. "Yeah, I'll live. One of the members of my group hacked into my code. It's damaged, but repairable.''

''Nasty, and illegal, as I'm sure you know,'' Winters said. ''Things going OK otherwise?''

''Oh, yeah,'' Maj said.

''Final exams for this year are coming up shortly, I believe,'' Winters said.

She gave him a brief sidelong glance. Winters kept surprisingly close tabs on the Net Force Explorers. It was an open secret that he intended to recruit some of them to full Net Force status when they were legal, or otherwise finished with whatever schooling they had planned for themselves.

Maj had also heard rumors from here and there that Net Force had covert ''scouts'' out in the virtual world, full-fledged Net Force agents in disguise, who spent their time looking around for suitable new talent, but she doubted that they were quite that sneaky about it, or needed to be. From her point of view, anybody with half a brain would want to belong to the organization that could tap into the coolest (or hottest) technology on the planet in its work—an organization whose members could go anywhere virtual, exploring a frontier that constantly expanded in front of them, managing and policing the most dangerous and fascinating aspect of modern life. Net Force agents had clout, and that was attractive—but even more so, to Maj, was the prospect of qualifying for a job in which, no matter what happened, you would never, ever be bored. At times like this, the prospect seemed more possible than usual . . . and that excited her.

But she was hardly going to show it. ''Finals? Yup,'' Maj said as casually as she could. ''I'm not overly concerned. Things are pretty much under control. I trust that my grade-point average meets your present standards?''

Winters grinned, but there was nothing even slightly sheepish about the look. ''There's always room to work harder, of course,'' he said . . . and his grin got wider as Maj gave him an ironic look. ''No, you're fine, I just like to keep an eye on everybody . . . make sure that the virtual end of life isn't strangling good old fashioned non-virtual reality. Balance—''

''—is everything,'' they finished together. ''So I hear,'' Maj said, ''repeatedly.'' Maj did not see Winters that often, either virtually or physically—he was a busy man—but that was the line he seemed to repeat at one point or another every time they met.

"Ahem," Winters said, and got up. "Yes. Well, you take care of yourself. That calculus grade slipped a little from last quarter."

Maj blinked, then gave Winters another dry look. The slippage would have coincided exactly with her period of heaviest work on the Valkyrie sim. "I don't think we'll have any more problems with that," she said. "The balance may swing . . . but it settles eventually."

Winters nodded. "Good to hear it," he said. "Do me a favor, though. When your sim's ready to fly again, let me know. I wouldn't mind watching it go over . . . hearing the roar."

"I'll do that," Maj said, oddly touched. The roar of the engines winding up—or down—was one of the things that got to her too.

"Right," Winters said. "My best to your folks." And he opened the door and was gone.

Maj just sat there for a moment, then shook her head. The man was like that—there and gone again, friendly but basically unrevealing, leaving you feeling afterwards, that there were ten or a hundred things that you should have said but didn't. Leaving you feeling evaluated—and desperately hoping that the evaluation had been a good one.

Her tea had gone cold. Maj got up and went over to one of the kitchen counters. She shoved the cup in the microwave and let it nuke itself for a minute, while she leaned against the sink and looked out the kitchen window at the birds hammering futilely on the bird table that stood out among the rose bushes in the back garden. Her mother resolutely refused to put seed or crumbs out for them this time of year, and walked around constantly muttering, "Let them eat bugs!" The caterpillars that kept getting at her roses were the bane of her existence, but she would use no chemical on them any stronger than liquid soap for fear of contaminating the local food chain. For her own part, Maj would have gone out to the local nursery and bought some tailored caterpillar predators, but Maj's mother insisted that that was what the birds were for. . . .

Bing! went the microwave. Maj retrieved her tea and went

back to sit down in the implant chair again. Only a few more pieces of mail. One was from Sander, another gossipy note full of complaints about Roddy, something obscure that he had heard about Roddy's new playroom, and some discussion of a new sim Sander himself was working on, something to do with the Akhoond of Swat, whatever that was.

Another one was from Roddy, purporting to do with his new sim. Maj "crumpled" it and chucked it away. Yet another one from Roddy: no text or voice or personal image in this one, just an associated file-tag that seemed to refer to a playroom location. Maj read the network address of the location and didn't recognize it. It wasn't Roddy's usual playroom address anyway. She raised her eyebrows. *If this is some dumb trick of his to get me to read an abusive mail,* she thought . . . and then curiosity got the better of her. After scanning it for everything she could think of—she didn't trust Roddy for some strange reason—she "unwrapped" the icon, telling it to display its content.

The kitchen and her workspace/villa both went away. Maj was standing in near-total darkness, with some kind of faint light source behind her. She put her hands out to something she could vaguely see in front of her, like a railing; no, a wall about waist height, made of something solid and cool, polished stone perhaps. *Well, this is dull,* she thought, and was about to turn around to see where the light behind her was coming from—

From above her, another source of light started to make itself noticeable. She glanced up . . . and gasped. Impossibly close, impossibly big, an eclipsed sun hung overhead, huge pale golden prominences arcing out from it and falling back into the unseen body of the star. A corona of unbelievable brilliance and detail leapt and streamed out from the blackness, and Maj thought she could hear a faint hissing and crackling in the air above, as if from an aurora. Impossible—

And then the sun stopped being totally eclipsed . . . a blinding crescent on the right-hand side of the sun appeared, and grew. Maj squinted, looking away instantly by reflex. It was dangerous to look at even so slight a bit of sun during an eclipse. But it became abruptly plain that this was not your usual eclipse. What should have been the shape of the moon

sliding off to one side was not: The shadow-shape, now re-
treating across the face of the sun, was straightening, the line
of its edge becoming less and less of a curve, as if it were no
sphere in front of the sun, but a spherical shell, or half a
spherical shell, rotating around the sunlike body. *Impossible*—

But it was happening. It was there. And below her, and all
around her, a landscape was becoming distinct as twilight
lifted. Far, far below, green fields, chains of mountains, rivers
winding oxbowed through many kinds of terrain . . . but all
miles below her. Maj was standing on a balcony, uplifted—
five miles? ten miles?—above that landscape. And it was not
flat. The land curved up around her on all sides. She squinted
upward from where the horizon should have been, and where
there was none; up, and up, until she was leaning her head
back, and still there was no end to the land, the rivers, even
lakes and seas. Right above her head they went, all the way
up and around to right behind the sun, or what passed for the
sun. Away on the other side of the world, darkness began to
sweep across the great hollow interior as the shell around the
sun rotated, and darkness fell where it blocked the light.

Maj remembered to breathe, and stood there, gazing up in
wonder, shaking her head. It was a hollow world, a Dyson
sphere perhaps: a whole solar system's worth of matter welded
together into a sphere with an artificial star inside . . . a world
with no sky, with nothing but more world everywhere you
looked, and the sun in the middle of it all. The balcony on
which she stood was part of a mountain. Maj leaned out over
the edge of it and looked down, and caught her breath again
at the sight of the whole mountain carved, intricately, gor-
geously, in strange alien-looking shapes and symbols, all a
great swirl of forms and textures reaching up to the balcony
where she stood. Behind her, as wonderfully carved, was the
door to a tunnel that led down into the mountain, and from
away down inside there, faint alien music rose.

The hair on the back of Maj's neck stood right up. She
turned back to look out at the bizarre and astonishing landscape, at the artificial sun above her head, and as the shell
rotated the rest of the way around it, leaving this side of the
hollow world bathed in light and the rest at darkness, burning
letters appeared in the air before her:

COME TO THE FUNHOUSE.

Maj breathed in and out a few more times, just taking in the amazing view . . . and then opened her hand, "dropping" the virt-mail with a gesture, crumpling it and tossing it aside. The white of her workspace, the brick and slate colors of the kitchen, reasserted themselves, the sun coming in the back window and hitting the oblivious Muffin's curls and setting every individual hair ablaze.

The icon of the mail sat on the table in front of her, an innocuous cube. Maj stared at it.

He may be a nasty little monster, she thought, *but my God, what a sim!*

There was another knock at the door "behind" her. Maj looked up. "Come in."

The door opened. Fergal stuck his head around it. "You busy?"

"Just doing the mail," she said, half relieved to have someone to talk to after what she had seen. "C'mon in."

Fergal sauntered in, looking around. "Nice day," he said. "Wish we could have weather like this all the time."

"If you're in Greece, you can," Maj said, and sighed a little. She would give a lot to exchange the heat and humidity of the D.C. area in summer for the sea-spray-flavored heat of the Greek islands. Virtuality aside, there was a specific charm to being there for *real* . . . and she had, once, for one memorable vacation, but her dad's salary didn't make that kind of thing possible very often.

Fergal sat down in the chair that Winters had vacated, and looked around at all the crumpled-up mail. "You too," he said.

"Oh, yeah," said Maj. "No change there."

The Muffin looked up from her book. "Maj, have you got *two* Invisible Friends?"

"No, honey," Maj said, amused. "Fergal is here, he's in my simming group and he just wanted to talk to me for a moment. Say hi to Fergal."

"Hi," the Muffin said, and turned her attention back to the book, making a one-handed wave at the "empty" chair without particularly looking at it.

"She says hello," Maj reported. "She thinks you're my Invisible Friend."

"Cute," Fergal said.

Maj smiled. "You wouldn't think it was so cute after her Invisible Friend had her spend an hour trying to get you to buy her a new doll when she already has about six hundred."

"Eight-six," the Muffin said from behind her book.

"Whatever!" Maj said. "Anyway"—and she turned her attention back to Fergal—"most of these virts are along the same lines. I am 'the worst in the world,' to quote Mr. L'Officier."

" 'The worst' at what?"

"Everything. You name it. But those aren't the mails I'm wondering about now." Maj reached out and uncrumpled the last one, so that the view of Roddy's new playroom would show again. Then she paused a moment and told her own virtual area to turn on a speech encrypter that would include her and Fergal, and keep any monitoring devices in Roddy's playroom from understanding them while they were "looking into" it. "Did you see this one?"

It unfolded around them. Fergal looked around as they stood on the balcony together. "Not this one specifically. A different view. But yeah . . . it's really something, isn't it?"

"Yeah," Maj said, rather unwillingly. "Fergal, how can he *do* stuff like this? His previous sims didn't look this good. Has he been holding out on us—or has he genuinely had some kind of breakthrough? Have we got a genuine genius in our midst?"

"Not in our midst at the moment," Fergal said, looking out into that astonishing view. "But if he is a genius, he's the kind that gives a bad name to geniuses everywhere. Unhinged . . . or just unsocialized. A menace."

"Maybe. I hate to say it," Maj said, looking out and down into the landscape, "but if he's doing stuff like this these days, whether he's been holding out on us or not, we really can learn things from him. And if that's the purpose of the Group . . ."

Fergal sighed. "You're not the only one to say that," he said after a moment.

Maj "dropped" the virt-mail. The kitchen and the villa

came back again. "So the Coventry consensus is cracking a little," Maj said. "Which is probably just what Roddy wants." She shook her head. "Fergal, if he gets what he wants, he wins. Not a good thing if we're trying to get him to clean up his act."

Fergal looked resigned. "You think anyone's likely to really do that," he said, "short of taking his brain out and doing a complete valve-and-ring job on it?"

Maj blinked. "Valve-and-ring—"

"It's an old car term," Fergal said. "See, valves were—"

"Never mind, I get the picture," Maj said. "Fergal, I don't know. But we're not going to do him much good if we're not consistent with him."

"I know. But Alain's been saying—"

"Oh, Alain," Maj said, and raised her eyebrows. "He's playing some kind of game with Roddy . . . or he thinks he is."

"Maj," Fergal said, "I know you're good with picking up what's going on with people. But do you actually have any evidence of this?"

"Uh," she said, and drank some of her tea, which was going cold again, "no."

"Maybe you should be careful about claiming stuff like that then," Fergal said.

Maj frowned. "I *am* careful about it. Anyway look, this is wonderful . . . dammit." She pushed the icon with one finger. "What are the others saying about it?"

"A couple of them have already been to this Funhouse thing," Fergal said. "Sander admitted as much to me."

She thought back to that rather covert reference in Sander's virt-mail to her referring to "Roddy's new little Funhouse." At the time, it had made little sense. "And who else?"

"Kelly. They both say it's just astonishing. That entire mountain is a mass of tunnels and galleries and caves apparently—it's got whole castles inside it, whole *cities* even, and all kinds of weird creatures. An incredibly beautiful piece of work."

"Did they go as themselves, or in other 'personas'?"

"Oh, disguised, of course."

Maj nodded, but she was willing to bet that Roddy had some

way of knowing exactly who was who regardless of spare personas or alternate virt-mail accounts. "I have to admit," she said, "I wouldn't mind having a look at it. . . ."

Fergal nodded. "A lot of the others have been saying the same," he said. "They want to do a Group look-through when this new playroom of Roddy's opens up officially tomorrow night. What about it? You want to come along?"

"Is the whole Group going to do this?" Maj said.

"I still have to poll Shih Chin and Mairead in person," Fergal said, "but I have mails from them that make it look like they're willing to go."

Maj rolled her eyes slightly. "Well, who am I to stand in the way of consensus?" she said. Fergal blinked, as if the irony had bit him a little harder than Maj intended.

"There are going to be thousands of people there apparently," Fergal said. "Invitations have gone out to moderators on all the main public simming groups, and there were blanket announcements in the unmoderated groups. It's going to be a huge event . . . and I think we can slip by unnoticed."

Maj had her own opinions about that. Yet at the same time, her conscience—she assumed it was her conscience—said, *Well, are you going to be unnecessarily petty and paranoid about this? If Roddy's really this talented, are you going to keep him from sharing his expertise and accomplishments with the Group just because he trashed your sim? Especially when they're all so eager to see what he's done?*

Phrased that way, the answer was obvious. *My problem,* Maj thought with great resignation, *is that I'm just no damn good at staying mad at people.* She wished she were more like her brother in this regard. Rick could hold a grudge until its hair turned gray and it begged to be let go to collect its old-age pension.

Maj sighed. "Okay," she said. "I'll go. I'm free tomorrow night fortunately. Where are we going to meet?"

"A public site," Fergal said. "I'll drop you the address. Roddy's playroom opens up at twenty hundred. We'll be fashionably late."

Maj nodded. "You're on," she said.

"Okay," Fergal said, and got up. "Have you got a spare persona?"

"Yeah," Maj said, "my dad has a couple of anonymized virtual accounts he keeps in case he needs them. He'll let me borrow one."

"Great. See you tomorrow at twenty then."

Fergal headed out the door, waved, and closed it behind him.

Maj put her chin down in her hands and stared at the glowing cubical icon sitting on the table in front of her.

"You're going cross-eyed," the Muffin observed from across the table. "They'll get stuck like that if you don't stop."

"Muffles," Maj said after a moment, "where do you hear stuff like that? Nobody's eyes are going to get stuck."

"Mom said it to Daddy yesterday," her sister said, carefully turning a page in her picture book. "Here it is, Maj! The archipelagus."

She held up the book proudly to show it to Maj. Maj peered at the winged shape illustrated there. "Oh. Muff, that's an *Archaeopteryx*."

"That's what I said," said Muffin, putting the book back down and turning the page with an air of great pleasure. "And here's the *Triceraplops*."

Maj smiled and got up to get herself one more cup of tea, but while the kettle was on the stove again, she looked at the little blue cube sitting on her side of the table . . . and again the hair stood up on the back of Maj's neck, and for no reason, she shivered.

5

In the darkness he sat and unwound the thread of destiny—
wound it together again, spliced it, and piled it up ready for
use.

It was dark in the hall of the Mountain King. He preferred
it that way. Roddy saved the light to be used to best effect.
Like most good creators, he did not have to see what he was
doing all the time to know what was going on.

Around him, in the dark, his creatures stirred and rustled.
He didn't have to see them either, and he knew they preferred
not to see him. He was a stern lord to his people, having many
important things to think about, more important things than
merely taking care of them or having their lives be easy.

After all, his life wasn't easy. Why should theirs be? It was
asking too much. And he had so much to do. . . .

Roddy pried apart the lysine and cytosine links in the strand
of DNA he was working on, and examined them, then reached
out into the darkness and came up with another strand, a loose
piece of messenger RNA that he had put aside earlier for this
use. He plugged it into place and let the strand reconstitute
itself, watching carefully as it did. While this part of the work
would progress quite nicely of its own accord if you let it,
you had to watch what it did. There were places and times
when you had to interfere with the rules for the interweave to
produce a specific effect . . . and specific effects were very
much what this piece of weaving was all about.

Roddy grinned to himself in the darkness—a straight line of a grin, with no curve of mirth about it.

Alain, he thought, *we'll see about you.*

It was tough to be a genius. It was even tougher when no one around you realized you were one. But worse still was when someone did . . . and decided that it might be nice to have a tame genius around. Useful . . . for their own purposes.

As if Roddy didn't have his own work to do . . . and his own ideas about what "useful" meant.

Barbarian, Roddy thought, and looked closely at the DNA to see how the strand had finished its reweaving. Then he ran a few more meters of it through his hands and found another spot that needed work.

"Nice," Alain had said when he came in to look around last time. Like some Goth wearing skins looking up at the ceiling of the Sistine Chapel and saying "nice." *He didn't have a clue,* Roddy thought. *Alain was sure he was on top of everything, though.*

That was going to change real quick.

And Alain had it coming. It was his fault, what the Group had done to Roddy. And Alain's idea for Roddy to get into Maj's sim and alter it a little. Well, more than a little. Alain didn't like Maj much, for some reason. Roddy didn't know or care why this might be. He found all of the Group unlikable most of the time, not that he took it out on them—they were fairly pathetic as it was, none of them terribly creative in the broader sense, or good at detail work.

But Maj had gone right to pieces after what was really a fairly elegant and well-constructed object lesson, and turned the Group against him. He still found it almost impossible to believe that she would have had the nerve to do anything but thank him for the lesson. Her obtuseness had astonished and infuriated him. And then Alain hadn't gotten the Group to understand what he'd done, what it had all been about . . . which had been Alain's job. After all, he went on all the time about how he was the only one who really understood Roddy. . . .

Well, both of them would find out soon enough that they were no match for him. But Alain first. All of this was his doing. He would be the first to pay.

And then, the rest of them, if they didn't see the error of their ways. If they did, if they had the sense to laugh, to acknowledge the cleverness of what he was going to do, then he would let them off.

Otherwise . . .

He ran the bright strands through his hands and found one more place that needed work. He pulled the sides of the DNA "ladder" apart, selected a couple of the rungs, and reached off to the side for another piece of messenger RNA to complete this piece. The molecule wove itself together as he watched, and the glow of the life-fire in it lit his face from beneath, shone in his eyes, shone through his hands. Out beyond the reach of the light, things scuttled and scuffed in the dark. He ignored them.

Viruses were not what they had been once upon a time. They'd started out as tricks and pranks, sometimes innocent, sometimes vicious: tiny self-replicating programs that could hide themselves in the empty parts of a disk drive and, when activated, play a little song, or type screenful after screenful of nonsense, or format "track 0" of the old-style hard drives and make the whole drive and all its data forever inaccessible, irretrievable, and useless.

Over time, as the computers became more complex and less likely to be understood by the people who were routinely using them, the viruses became more complex as well, and harder to find even for those who understood the nature of the machine language in which they might be written, the computer version of a biological virus's "genetic code." A fragment of computer virus would secrete itself somewhere in a computer's memory, move from place to place in the solid storage, kill a bit of data here, a byte there, otherwise leaving no trace of its passage until the system began to malfunction because of those tiny losses of pieces of program or data.

After that the complexity of computer viruses began to be a wonderful thing, the creators of the viruses always one step ahead of those who made it their business to find and stop them. It was an elegant mirroring of the actions of virulent organisms in the real world, as one by one the bacteria and viruses and rickettsiae and other tiny creatures that preyed on more complex living things themselves became slowly resistant to the chemicals that had so long been used successfully against them.

It had occurred to Roddy—oh, maybe a couple of years ago, when he was first starting to get involved in simming—that mirroring could be carried much further, the symmetry running down into the roots of the virtual world as well as into the depths of the physical one. If a computer virus could make a computer sick—then surely, if you were careful and thoughtful, you could find a way to make a computer user's persona sick.

Virtuality was all about the interface between the mind and the physical, after all, or the mind and the nonphysical. At that interface, where the concrete body met the virtual one, there could certainly be some way for virtuality to directly affect the body where the mind lived. That there didn't seem to be one now didn't bother him. Even the present effects of virtuality on the body were impossible thirty years ago. And now, when you road-raced at Le Mans in a virtual car, your pulse went up, didn't it? Your body chemistry changed, hormones were pumped out into your system, exactly as they would if you were genuinely coming around the Grand Chicane. Stimulus and response . . . except that the stimulus was virtual.

So . . . couldn't there be other ways to stimulate virtually? Other parts of the body to be influenced and triggered, other mechanisms to manipulate? The thought had fascinated Roddy. He wasn't interested in gross physical movement or stimulation, the simple kind of stuff that went on in Net sites where people got involved in what were supposed to be the safest kinds of physical relationships, or did mountain climbing, or other such straightforward things. What fascinated Roddy was the mind-body interface, where the old saying "mind over matter" had its original source. Matter affected mind by such methods as neurotransmitter chemicals and hormones. Mind affected matter by causing the body to produce those chemicals. And the experience of the mind, finally, was virtual. It experienced nothing directly. Everything was filtered through the senses, even as virtual experience had to come to the mind via the computer interface's manipulation of those senses.

So, if the mind could produce chemicals like adrenaline,

could it be convinced to produce other chemicals, from the basic raw materials available? Not the usual ones, not the normal ones, but new chemicals, new compounds?

Maybe even new organisms?

It was a pretty problem. People had spent a long time arguing over whether viruses or rickettsiae were actually "alive." Granted, they acted as if they were. They reproduced themselves, they respired in a primitive way, they reacted to stimuli. But that was about all they did. As chemicals went, they were geniuses. As organisms went, they were abysmally stupid. But not so stupid that they hadn't assembled themselves out of raw materials.

Roddy found himself wondering whether, using only virtual tools—bits of programming, strands of code—you could build something that was genuinely, virtually alive. Not the fake kind of life that was all that even the best virtuality involved. No matter how solid the stuff around you felt, no matter how warm the flesh or blue the sky, it was all code in the end. What Roddy wanted to create was code that would get loose in virtuality and take care of itself—respire, react to stimuli . . . breed. And eventually . . . become complex enough to become an organism. The equivalent of single-celled, at first. Then multiple-celled. Then later . . .

He had no idea what might eventually come of this work. A genuinely new and different life form, he thought: something that would move through virtuality like a fish through water, independent, intelligent.

He would be a creator. He would be a father. Something that genuinely lived would look at him and say, *Maker.*

Of course, ethical programmers wanted nothing to do with this kind of thing. Ethical programmers were cowards. They were on the edge of a tremendous discovery, and they shied away from it, terrified of what might happen.

Some were not so terrified. Oh, Roddy didn't intend to hurt anybody. Or not much. But at the same time, he intended to find out what the ethical types dared not. He would have to be careful. Anyone who suspected what he was working on would probably try to stop him.

But in the meantime, he would keep working. He would do

his initial experimental work, keeping careful records of the results.

He was fortunate in having someone to experiment on.

In the darkness, Roddy sat in the stone chair, passing the strand of life through his hands, and smiled. There was no one to pass it to, at the moment.

But there would be shortly. . . .

The next evening, Maj wandered into the room furthest back in the house, next to the garage. They called it the "den," though it was more a kind of all-purpose room that the family used for reading and working on anything that wasn't too messy. All the furniture that was too beat-up to keep elsewhere in the house, but too comfortable or well-liked to get rid of, had gravitated there. Her brother was there too, a long gangly shape with close-cropped dark hair, waving his arms around as he lay back in the VR chair with his feet up, apparently talking earnestly on the portable video phone. He was going on about "skips" and "vice-skips" and "bonspiels" and "takeouts" and "sheets" at a great rate, which meant he was having a discussion with somebody about curling.

Maj was tempted to snicker, but restrained herself. Rick had once described curling to her as "a profoundly inward experience of the intersection of motion and time." *Throwing a smooth rock across the ice and running around in front of it with a broom,* Maj thought. *"Profoundly inward." Huh.* But then this was Rick, who had once described the behavior of a newly acquired pitcher for the Orioles as "Nietzchean." Maj frequently wondered which planet had smuggled her brother onto Earth as a part of what peculiar genetic engineering experiment. Her father claimed that Rick was probably the milkman's fault, but Maj privately doubted that the milkman had the genetic complement to be responsible.

She stepped over and touched Rick's shoulder. "Hey, listen," she said, "have you seen my jacket?"

"Uh." He blinked. "In the laundry room, hanging up. I think Mom was tidying again."

"Okay." She wandered off to get it. By the time she got back, Rick was finished with his call and standing up, stretching until his joints cracked. He looked over at her with an expression that reminded her once again of an owl's: bemused, slightly cockeyed, but potentially dangerous. "Going out?" he said.

"Yeah."

"Meeting somebody?"

"Not physically."

He blinked again. "Virtual? Then why go out?"

"I want to use a public linkage site," she said. "Less obvious . . ."

"You could always run your input from here through a bottom-level anonymizer."

"Some people would find that all too obvious," Maj said.

"Oh," Rick said then, "I get it. You're gonna go read Mr. Hacker the riot act?"

Maj made a wry face. "I wish someone would," she said, "but no, I'm not going to waste my time. Instead we're all going off to look at his new playroom."

"That 'Funhouse' thing?"

"You've heard about it?" Maj was surprised. Rick had no particular interest in simming.

Rick nodded. "Been some publicity on the virt-news channels," he said. "They say it's supposed to be pretty involved."

Maj nodded. "From the glimpse I had, I'd believe it."

"Well, tell me all about it when you get back," her brother said, heading out of the den and toward his room down the hall. "But it's a shame no one can arrange to crash *his* big fancy sim now that the little firk's going public with it."

"Uh—" Maj said.

"Well," Rick said from down the hallway, "if you need someone pulverized afterwards, let me know. . . ." His voice trailed off as his room door closed behind him.

"I don't know if pulverizing's legal," Maj said to the hallway, but she smiled. Trust Rick to say the things she wouldn't say no matter how hard she thought them.

It took her about twenty minutes by public transport to get down to the second-most-convenient of two public sites near her house—Maj half wondered whether Roddy would have some kind of bug in the nearer of the two. The place was

comfortable enough—a small shopfront in a minimall, between a Chinese restaurant and a pet store—and she knew the
people who ran it. Maj did her credit check-in, took a key for
a booth, closed herself in, got comfortable in the extremely
expensive and modern implant chair, and lined her implant up.
Things dimmed as she started to slip into the Net. She briefly
resisted the urge to hiccup, as always happened—

—and the world went virtual around her, resolving to the
rather neutral ''immediate'' space of the public site: eggshell-
beige walls, sourceless lighting, and empty air. Maj fed the
public space the coordinates for her own workspace. Immediately her surroundings were replaced by the whites and
brushed steels of her workspace.

Maj kept the ''villa'' on Athens time. It might be dark in
Alexandria, Virginia, but early light was already turning the
sky indigo over the Peloponnese peninsula, and through the
skylight it was apparent that rosy-fingered dawn was bearing
down on the Greek islands with intent.

She went over to one of the filing cabinets built into the
wall and pulled it open, looking through the various icons and
representations of on-line resources that she kept stored there.
The cabinet was not very organized. Right now it was organized like one of the Muffin's toy chests, full of blocks and
pyramids and spheres and various other miniatures of ''real''
objects, all representing places or services available in the virtual world. Something stuck her in the hand as she was rooting
around. ''Ow,'' she said. ''Ow, ow,'' as it stuck her again
while she grabbed it and pulled it out. It was a small model
of the Taj Mahal. ''What the heck,'' she said, and shook the
icon to ''unwrap'' its virtual content.

Immediately jangly sitar music surrounded her, with a
strong smell of something spicy cooking. A tall man in a tur-
ban bowed to her, with his hands together in a prayerful position, and said, ''Ten percent off on your next meal at the
Al-Akbar Restaurant, Falls Church, Virginia. For reservations
link to—''

Maj chuckled and flipped the icon so that it would rewrap
itself, then dropped it back in the cabinet. *Must give that to
Mom to add to the virtual coupon collection.* She reached right
down to the bottom of the cabinet and finally came up with

what she was looking for: an ornate half-mask, gilded and feather-trimmed, the kind of thing one would have worn to the great Masked Ball in Venice, in the days when "La Serenissima" was still the city-empire that ruled the seas.

She lifted it up and turned it this way and that in the subdued evening lighting of her workspace, admiring the glint of the gold. It wasn't a real mask, of course. It was a symbol for a virtual identity. Putting it on immediately channeled your own virtual persona's information through an upper-level anonymizer, so that another person using the Net couldn't "recognize" you, or use an analysis program to find out important or potentially private information about you. This kind of "light" anonymizer would attract a lot less attention from people (like Roddy) who would be looking for evidence that someone was presenting this virtual persona from their own site, trying to hide its location as well as their own identity.

There was of course no way to conceal the fact that you were using an anonymizer—most of both the public and private networks required at least that much disclosure—but that by itself wasn't terribly unusual. Lots of people preferred to keep almost all their virtual business private, usually on the grounds that there were too many ways to find out too much about people as it was. Even governments could not always be trusted to use personal information appropriately. In the final analysis, governments were made up of private persons . . . and they were as likely to misuse or overuse confidential information as anyone else.

Maj shook her hair back and put the mask on. It needed no strings or other fastenings. It would stay there until she wanted it to come off. For additional protection, and because it amused her, she would now look like her brother. She glanced down to check her appearance, and saw that she was indeed wearing his very beat-up jeans, and a T-shirt that said SAS-KATCHEWAN CURLING CLUB.

"Right," she said softly, hoping desperately that no one asked her any questions about curling. She wouldn't know a bonspiel if one came up to her and bit her in the knee.

Maj "backed out" of her site and made sure her virtual identity was in order, then gave the public site the "address" of the Group of Seven's scheduled meeting place, which Fergal had sent to her. A door opened before her in the air. She stepped through it.

On the other side of it was a broad wooden porch attached to a big old white-shingled house of resolutely Down East architecture, the kind of place you might expect to find around Cape Cod. Indeed, that was where this location seemed to be. Step off the porch and you would be standing on a lawn of short, coarse salt grass, which suddenly grew longer at the edge of the ''yard'' and began sloping down to the dunes of a nearby beach. Sitting around in various wicker chairs and on various pieces of beat-up porch furniture were the other members of the Group of Seven.

At least Maj assumed that was who they were, since as far as she knew nobody else was expected to be in this particular subdivision of this particular public site at the moment. The trouble was that, since everyone was wearing virtual identities, they were all unrecognizable: a group of wildly assorted people, male, female, young, old, and in a couple of cases, not even human—there was one shocking pink pony with a long purple mane, and a large and mournful-looking orangutan.

''God,'' Maj said, ''maybe we should have name tags.''

''Or red carnations or something,'' Alain said. He looked like an unusually good-looking young woman in tight Nu-Slicks with long blond hair, but as yet he hadn't added a filter to change the sound of his voice: The effect was unusual.

Fergal guffawed. ''If you keep your voice like that, you won't need a carnation. Maybe we should all just keep our voices the way they are.''

''Don't know if that's such a good idea,'' Maj said. ''If I know Roddy, he's got listeners installed all over this sim to see if our voices show up.''

''Much as I hate to admit it,'' Sander said, ''she's probably right. What are we going to do about this?''

''I've got a little 'cone-of-silence' program,'' Maj said, ''or not really silence. It's an on-the-fly packet encrypter for private speech communication. We can talk freely among ourselves, and it'll be a lot more trouble and processing time than anyone can spend to find out what we're saying before next week or so. But for visual identification—''

''Secret decoder rings?'' Mairead said.

Eyebrows were raised at this. "Good enough," Kelly said. "We can all wear matching ones . . . and keep our hands in our pockets when we get separated, if we have to."

It was as good an idea as any. They settled on a plain class-ring style with a cabochon-cut green stone. "One other thing," Mairead said as they all materialized the rings, "it might be good to put 'joy buzzers' in them. A vibrating alert function . . . it buzzes when the person next to you has one of the rings on, so you know you're talking to one of us."

They agreed on a frequency and enabled the buzzers. "Okay," Bob said, "where now?"

"Back to our original public-access sites," Kelly said. "We'll come in in a few small groups, as Fergal suggested earlier. Everybody have their set of coordinates for the entry area for Roddy's reception area?"

Everyone nodded. Everyone vanished. Maj backed up to her public site again, fed it the coordinates—

—and instantly found herself in a vast stony atrium lit by huge glowing alabaster globes, hanging from a ceiling so high that they couldn't see it. Off to one side Maj saw Fergal, and moved toward him casually. "Those are *clouds* up there," Fergal said. "Get a load of—"

Sander joined them a few moments later. "This place must be a mile across," Sander whispered to Fergal. "How the heck has he—"

"Welcome to the Funhouse," said a pleasant voice, and a creature came over to them. It was tall and very thin, with pearly skin and no hair, looking like a cross between an alien of the kind once called "grays" and someone's idea of what elves should look like. It handed them each a small token, a square tablet of blue glass about an inch across. "Here is your map. Refreshments to the right, adventures to the left, scenery and the ballroom straight ahead. Enjoy your visit."

It wandered away to greet some more new arrivals. The three of them paused to look at their maps. Then Sander whispered, to Maj this time, "See the others?"

"Yeah, they're across there, the first group—and there's the second. That's all of us. Let's sort ourselves out the way we had it arranged before, and go in."

The others heard this via their private communications "cir-

cuit'' and nodded, mingling with the crowd a little and ther
sorting themselves into a group of two and two other groups
of three each. Maj put herself with Shih Chin, currently in the
shape of a large handsome black guy with astonishing muscles
and a perfectly tailored three-piece suit, and Mairead, who was
hitching herself expertly along the floor as the orangutan. Ma
put her thumbnail into the activating slot for the token, and
the map unfolded itself in the air before her, in three dimensions, and followed her as she went.

"A hundred and fifty levels," she said softly. "Each one
three miles by five, give or take a quarter mile here and there."

"It *can't* be that big," Chin said, looking around her, but
doubt was showing in her voice already, though it sounded
strange hearing it about three octaves lower than normal.

"Tell Roddy that," Maj said. "Look here—here's something called the 'central atrium'—should we try that first?"

"Sounds as good as anything else."

They walked on through the immense hall. There were quite
a few people here, maybe a thousand or so in this space alone.
Many of them were just normal people walking around and
chatting with the aliens and strange creatures populating the
space, not all of which were Roddy's constructs by any stretch
of the imagination. A lot of people liked to "dress up" for a
big virtual event, and so there were a lot of people in costume.
At least Maj doubted that there were *this* many cosmetically
perfect specimens in the non-on-line world, this many drop-
dead-gorgeous women, this many staggeringly handsome men.
Well, she thought, *no harm in dolling yourself up a little for
a big night out.*

But there were a lot of people who had taken the idea of
"costume" a little more seriously, and so strolling around on
the shining stone floor there were barbarians in loincloths, and
numerous versions of characters from popular virtual entertainments, old and new: the villain from the latest Bond movie
was there about twenty times, and so were many unlikely creatures from pre-stereo entertainment. Maj had been slightly embarrassed by Bob's little pink horse with the long silky mane,
until she was nearly run over by a very fast long-legged bird,
with some kind of tall skinny dog chasing after it with an ai

of determined desperation. Plainly the loonies were out in force tonight.

She paid more attention, though, to the aliens that seemed to be Roddy's creation: mostly very tall slender creatures like the one that had greeted them, astonishingly graceful and handsome, and with amazing variation among them. This was no stamped-out, templated bunch of constructs. Real care and work had gone into all these people. One group of them went by dressed in gorgeous embroidered clothes that reminded Maj of medieval Russian formal robes, crusted with gems and gold lace. They were playing stringed instruments, and singing, a strange melody that seemed to combine aspects of classical chamber music and early twentieth-century discordance . . . with other influences that Maj couldn't recognize.

I wouldn't have thought he had this in him, Maj thought. *Delicacy, beauty. But then it just goes to show you how wrong you can be about people. Or no—not wrong, but your knowledge can be very incomplete.*

She sighed as she and her small group walked along toward an immense opening in the stone wall ahead of them. Or at least some of them walked. She edged a little closer to her companion on her right, and whispered, "Mairead—why the orangutan?"

The orang gave Maj a thoughtful look as she swung along. After a moment she said, "It's a natural redhead . . . *but no one ever asks.*"

"Ouch," Maj said.

The crowd was building up a little in front of them. The groups from the Seven slowed, then drifted together a little, pushed there by the crowd that was gathering in front of something that Maj couldn't see. Slowly then, the crowd parted to either side, and started to disperse down a great curving flight of stairs on each side. Directly in front of Maj and Mairead and Chin was a railing of graceful stone columns. They walked up to it and looked over and down to the main floor.

"My gosh," Maj said.

"Great Buddha on a bicycle," said Shih Chin.

"Ook," said Mairead, in complete astonishment.

"Thousands of people" might have been an understatement. It looked like there were about *ten* thousand people in here ... and the amazing thing was, this space had room to hold them all. The central "atrium" of this area rose up eight stories above, and each level appeared to have about fifty acres worth of arched and galleried spaces stacked in it. People were everywhere, examining the ornate wall-carvings, talking to the aliens, and generally just being amazed at the place.

They had reason. "I can't believe this," Kelly said to Maj at one point as they made their way down the great broad polished stone stairs toward the bottom level and Kelly came away from a wall she had been examining. "None of this is authored stuff, by the usual definition," she said quietly. "None of it is supported-boundary technique or Potemkin surfaces or anything. It's all *grown* somehow. No fractals, no cheating ... everything's been done molecule by molecule, it looks like. As if it were real. How's he *doing* this?"

Maj shook her head. "He's a genius," she said, though admitting it made her feel like she was having to eat whole lemons.

Their groups drifted together again as they came down to the main floor, and they strolled on, trying not to look too closely associated, but also trying not to lose one another. This level of the atrium led into yet another through one more huge archway ... and as they passed through the vast doorway that let onto the next atrium, everyone goggled. The next atrium was *bigger* than the last one, the central space easily a mile across.

"It's not fair," Alain muttered behind Maj as they started across the echoing expanse of the bottommost floor, while groups of strolling alien players went by strumming on various instruments and singing in high sweet voices. "Where's he putting it all?"

Everyone shook their heads.

"It's a fair question," Maj said, under her breath, to Shih Chin. "And more to the point, how's he *affording* all this? To erect this kind of virtual structure you need hundreds of thousands of dollars worth of storage."

"It's not so much a question of that," Chin said, looking around her. "He really hasn't spent that much—I had a look at his playroom specs before I came in. He published them. Oh, it wasn't cheap ... but he's not paying for any more space han you've got, or I have. What he seems to have done is found a way to compress all this content into a space that takes only a tenth of what it *looks* like it should. He's not just using composition software. He must be writing directly in VirtC++ or one of the other machine languages, packing the information down as tight as it *can* be packed.''

Maj shook her head again, in what was turning into a very persistent and repetitive action. This was all genuinely astonishing work—far above the level that any of them had managed in their own simming so far; and in Maj's estimation, it was better than some professional sims out there on the Net that cost serious money to get into. This whole setup was more than some little attempt by Roddy's to impress the group—much more. This was a calling card, an announcement to the world at large and to the simming community in particular that he was now officially on the scene and he was going to be a force to be reckoned with. The virtuosity of the message was galling . . . and Maj couldn't help but admire it. *I just hope this level of accomplishment is enough to overcome the way he deals with people,* she thought, *because if it's not . . .*

But she had the idea that it would be. That idea was reinforced when, about an hour later, after much more wandering through the carven mountain, and then out through extraordinary vistas under that selectively eclipsing sun, they came back into the mountain and ran across Roddy himself. He was standing directly under the highest point of a huge dome apparently carved out of a single massive lump of marble, but it was some kind of marble that generated light, so that the whole thing glowed with a cool white radiance that was easy on the eyes and at the same time quite strange. He was wearing an old-fashioned tuxedo, with a red bow tie, red piping-trim on the lapels, and red socks. In a cockeyed sort of way, he looked splendid. Roddy was surrounded by what appeared to be a large number of media people—some of them carrying their press credentials visibly, others simply listening, though doubtless every word Roddy said was going into a recording site somewhere else and would be all over the news tomorrow. Roddy was not missing the opportunity. He was talking a mile a minute, and the media people were hanging on his every word.

"Look at him," Shih Chin rumbled softly. "He's lapping it right up."

"Wouldn't you?" Maj asked.

"No argument."

They walked by without stopping or seeming to be particularly interested, at least no more so than would be indicated by the appropriate glance at the happy form in the tux. That was maybe what surprised Maj more than anything else. Roddy looked *genuinely* happy. It wasn't that nasty little "I'm going to get you somehow" smile that he so routinely wore. Yet the difference somehow bothered Maj too, and she couldn't tell why.

Certainly not anything as routine and awful as jealousy, her conscience remarked. *Certainly you wouldn't begrudge anyone else all this attention. He'll be famous by this time tomorrow. People will be crawling all over him to make deals with him. Certainly that can't be bothering you.*

Maj hated it when her conscience took such a sarcastic tone with her. Yet perhaps the sarcasm was deserved.

They went on by, and headed in the general direction of an alcove a few hundred feet off to one side where something smelled good. "Food," Fergal said, "that's a thought. . . ."

"That's *always* a thought for you," Kelly said.

"Oh, come on now," said Fergal as they made their way to a groaning silk-draped banquet table where more of Roddy's aliens, somewhat incongruously dressed in chefs' whites and toques, were serving everything from Beluga caviar to what were plainly slices from a whole roast ox with gilded horns and hooves. "I haven't mentioned food," Fergal said, "in, oh . . ."

"Five minutes," said the small pink pony with the long purple mane.

"Oh, go find yourself some hay," said Fergal, and picked up a plate.

So did most of them, except for Maj, who'd eaten late and wasn't hungry, and Bob, of course, who in his pony state couldn't hold a plate. He went over to the salad bar and had a chat with a most accommodating elf-alien. Shortly thereafter he was munching on an artistically arranged mixed salad, heavy on the alfalfa sprouts, while Fergal and Alain and Kelly and the others either worked their way up and down the serve-yourself buffet, hitting the caviar and the blinis and the many other delicacies laid out there, or waited for the team of chefs to carve them off a serving or two of roast beast.

"He can cook," Sander said, shaking his head. "You've got to give him that."

Maj started to shake her head again, then stopped herself, determined not to do it any more tonight. Next to her, Mairead was working her way through a kiwi and orangelle fruit salad dressed in carambola vinaigrette. "This is great," she said. "I've got to get the recipe."

"I'm sure he'll be delighted to give it to you," Maj said, glancing out toward the main part of the hall again. Roddy was still standing there surrounded by people who were interviewing him. She could barely see his head through the crowd gathered around him.

She breathed out, turned back to the buffet table, and eyed the blinis. The sour cream looked good. As she moved toward it, she saw Alain looking at Roddy too. Then he turned away. "Woo hoo," Alain said, apparently apropos of nothing.

Maj looked over at Fergal, who was digging into a plateful of German potato salad, and raised her eyebrows. Fergal glanced at Alain, then back at Maj, and shrugged. Alain's sense of humor could occasionally be a little strange, but then they all had weird moments. It wouldn't do to get Shih Chin, for example, started on one of her riffs about Bolivian alternative comedy. *Especially not when she's dressed as a man,* Maj thought. *The confusion—*

"Yes," Alain said, rather loudly, and then, "So what're you all looking at?" he shouted, in a tone of voice that seemed to be cheerful, but which the shouting made strange. His sheer volume startled all the members of the Group a little. They turned to look at him, for he seemed not to have been shouting at them, but at one of Roddy's aliens. "Isn't this the damnedest thing you ever saw? Doesn't it just make you want to bite your own head off?"

The whole Group exchanged bemused glances. Everyone else congregated in the food area was also looking at Alain. He seemed oblivious. He carried on shouting, louder than before, so loudly that his voice began to crack when he did it.

"Something else," he said, still in a conversational way, but at a volume that Maj thought would bid fair to crack glass. In this huge space, the echoes traveled, so that fragments of words came back a second later. The group out in the main part of the hall, around Roddy, was turning to look now.

"Just an amazing—" Alain shouted. Then he began to sing at the top of his not-inconsiderable lungs. "I am—the king— of a western land—and I hold—the box—of green—"

It was no tune or song that Maj had ever heard before. All around Alain a kind of bewitched silence was falling. Even Roddy's graceful and seemingly imperturbable aliens were staring. The silence spread, broken only by Alain's yodeling— there was now no other word for it.

"Has he been drinking?" Maj heard someone whisper.

She shook her head one last time. It didn't seem to matter, for drunk or sober, Alain plainly couldn't carry a tune in a bucket. He apparently couldn't manage to carry his plate either. He dropped it, busy waving his arms. The bone china shattered on the floor, and caviar and sliced breast of pheasant and Cumberland sauce went everywhere. "And when I saw— the beast with a thousand heads—" It wasn't a song anymore. It was a rant, and Alain had begun staggering around the place, windmilling his arms, so that people started backing away from him hurriedly when he came close to them.

The Group members drew together as if magnetized by the bizarreness of what was happening. "What's the *matter* with him?" Bob said, astounded.

Sander put his plate down. "I don't know, but—"

"The beast," Alain yelled, "it wants—everything, it wants—" The staggering was getting more uncoordinated. Maj saw the sweat burst out on Alain's forehead with great suddenness, and as it did so, his virtual persona fell off, so that he wasn't disguised anymore, but was palpably Alain, palpably out of control, lurching around, his eyes glazing and the pupils looking dilated and fixed, his face suddenly fixed too, in a sort of long unsmiling rictus. He didn't seem to be able to move his head, and it stayed as still as if he was wearing a neck brace, though all the rest of him now seemed to be trying to go in all directions at once.

"It sits in the dark, and it weaves its webs, and we're all—

we're—Alone! Isolated! Isolationism! Free silver! I can't—free—''

His legs tangled themselves together somehow. He went down. Bob was there first, catching him across the back of the pony-shape. By the time the first part of the fall was broken, Sander and Kelly had rushed in and caught Alain, easing him the rest of the way to the floor, once shining but now spattered with food and scattered with broken china. Alain lay there stiff-necked, jerking, trying to say things but suddenly unable to do anything but make strangled noises.

''He's gone spare,'' Fergal said in astonishment, the Yorkshire accent coming out much more clearly than usual.

''He's sick,'' Maj said, though at first she had been ready enough to agree with Fergal. But this did not look like any kind of ''normal'' craziness to her, and she felt a sudden terrible pity for Alain in the face of all the eyes gathered around them, all those staring, curious eyes. ''Come on, let's get him out of here!''

The rest of the group gathered around him. ''Where does he live?''

''He's in New York someplace. Get the address, let's call his house, see if there's someone there who can help—''

''I've got their link number,'' Fergal said. ''It's sounding—''

He stood vacant-eyed for a moment, while the others stood staring at him and at Alain, now twitching vaguely on the floor and muttering, ''A banner—banner with a strange—device—''

''No answer,'' Fergal said after a moment. ''No one home but him. Their answering service came on—''

''Call the paramedics,'' Maj said. ''He's sick—''

People were gathering around them, muttering, staring. ''Come on,'' Maj said to Kelly, ''back to your playroom, quick!'' She knelt down beside Alain to check his pulse. It was fast. He was feverish—the hand with which she felt his forehead came away dripping with sweat.

Kelly threw open a door in the air. The others grabbed Alain, levered him up between them, and pulled him through the doorway. Last through the door was Maj, and as she pulled it closed behind her, across the great crowded room she suddenly saw one more pair of staring eyes. They belonged to

Roddy. They were looking at her with the same expression she had half-seen on his face when she'd said, *He's sick.* Roddy's normal smile was back again—the one with the angry, cheerful curl at the edges of it. The one that said, *Gotcha.*

6

It was a very late night for Maj after she got home again—not because she didn't want to sleep, but because she couldn't. She watched dawn come up, not in Greece but in Alexandria, Virginia, and as soon as she decently could, before she would have to leave for school, she went into her workroom and told it to link her to Net Force. A moment later, she was standing in James Winters's office. The first light of morning was shining in through the blinds, patterning the piled-up papers on the desk. Winters looked at Maj, past the papers and what was apparently his first cup of coffee, judging by his slightly bleary look, and said, "To what do I owe the pleasure?"

She told him. It took a while. Winters did nothing while he listened but nod once or twice, while Maj paced up and down and related everything in order. At the point where isolationism and free silver had begun to be mentioned, Maj finally had to stop.

"Something to drink?" Winters said.

"Tea, please," Maj said, "if you've got it. But—Mr. Winters, he went out of his head. Just completely cuckoo. Incoherent, uncoordinated. We broke the whole group out of the sim and called his house. I couldn't get an answer—so another of our crew called the emergency services. They told us that the paramedics broke in and found him unconscious . . . and since then we haven't heard anything."

"You don't have any contacts with his parents?"

Maj shook her head. "We tried to reach them last night. They weren't home."

Winters looked unfocused for a moment as he gazed off to one side, checking some data that was visible to him but not to Maj, and blinking a few times, apparently sorting through a set of menu options as they appeared. "Thurston?" he said. "14-302 Ocean Parkway, Brooklyn?"

"That's it."

"He's in Cornell Medical Center in Manhattan," Winters said. "The short public-level bulletin says he was in intensive care until this morning, but they've downgraded him to a normal ward for observation for tonight . . . apparently whatever treatment they used on him must have worked."

"What was the matter with him?"

"This listing won't say. Confidentiality. Half a second." There was a pause, and Winters looked toward the Venetian blinds on his window and said to the air in that direction, "Hi, Magda. James Winters at Net Force. Yes, how are you? Long time no see. Listen, Magda, I need a release on a diagnosis, someone's class-2'd it because the subject was a minor admitted unaccompanied. Yeah. Thurston, Alain. That's right. Yes, pre-investigation. I'm trying to rule something out." He paused a moment more, then said, "Thanks, Magda."

Winters turned back to Maj, and got up. He went to the office door and opened it. A tray with a cup of tea was sitting outside. He brought it in and handed it to Maj. "This is of course confidential," he said. "They diagnosed him as having a noncontagious meningeal inflammation, probably secondary to a systemic infection."

"What kind?"

"Nonspecific."

"I'm not so sure about the 'nonspecific,' " Maj said, grim. "I'm sure this is something that Roddy did to him."

Winters sat back in his chair. "Did *how*?"

"I don't know," Maj said. "But I'm sure of it." She stopped, and then said, because she felt she had to, "And I don't have any proof."

Winters sighed and folded his arms. "Our society," he said, "bought into the infallibility of concrete proofs and science and logic a long time ago . . . and it sold uncertainty and instinct and intuition and hunches down the river as a result. Made them disreputable . . . until we're ashamed to even admit having them. Even when they work.'' He frowned. ''The scientific method is a fad. A useful one . . . but hardly the only way to get things done. Heaven only knows what we'll be using two hundred years from now.'' Winters sighed. ''Meanwhile, don't discount your hunches. But this leaves us with a problem. How do you virtually give someone an actual infection? It can't be done.''

''*Yet*,'' Maj said. ''I saw him doing some other stuff that can't be done either. Or can be done, but not without tons of money and hundreds of people. How's *he* doing them?''

Winters nodded. ''It's a fair question,'' he said. ''Tell you what . . . have you run into Mark Gridley lately?''

''Uh, no, I don't see him that much outside of Net Force Explorer meetings.''

''No, I know you don't, but he was at this opening the other night as well. I didn't know if you might have met up with him or not. If you think this is something to do with strictly virtual structures—not to malign your own talent in this area, which is plainly considerable, but—''

''Believe me, I don't feel particularly maligned,'' Maj said. ''What Roddy was doing just about everywhere else in that sim was *way* over my head. If you think Mark might have a take on this that would do some good, I'd love to talk to him. I may not like Alain much, but he's part of my group—and after what I saw the other night, I don't think I like the idea of it happening to anybody else.''

''No,'' Winters said, ''I can see that. Shall I tell Mark to call you then?''

''Sure.''

''And what if you're wrong?''

Maj put the teacup down. ''Then I'm wrong,'' she said. ''But isn't it better to investigate, and be sure, than rule something out because it's 'impossible' . . . and then find that it's not?''

Winters smiled very slightly. ''After you eliminate the impossible,'' he said, ''what remains must be the truth. But you're right. The elimination is the sticky part.'' He picked up his coffee cup, had a drink, made a face, and set it aside. "Get busy . . . and tell me what you find."

Alain got out of the hospital feeling much better . . . physically, at least. But when he got home, the days that followed made him wish that he could have stayed in the hospital a while longer.

His parents, for one thing, were sure that his attack had actually been caused by Alain doing some kind of drugs. The explanations of the doctors and nurses that he had genuinely been sick made no impact whatever on his folks . . . possibly because none of the medical people were able to explain where he had picked up the abrupt and acute infection that had caused the meningitis, and his associated brief bout of dementia. Their statement to his parents that they had in fact ruled out any drug abuse simply suggested to his father (who had finally found out what Alain's grades really were, after an unexpected meeting with his advisor) that Alain had found some way to hide what he had been up to, even from the experts.

As a result, home life had become a little hell. His father wasn't talking to him except in monosyllables, and his allowance was stopped. His mother was doing the "wounded to the quick" act, which mostly involved looking at him with an expression that suggested she had somehow raised him badly, that being the only reason he could have acted this way. The near-hourly sighs of "How *could* you, Alain" were beginning to get on his nerves, most particularly because he *hadn't*. Well, he had about the grades . . . but there was no getting either of them to understand about that. Not now . . .

For his Net life was essentially over.

I can't go back, he thought. *I have no* idea *why I did what I did. I went nuts. I acted nuts in front of everybody.*

I'll die of embarrassment if any of them see me again.

It took another couple of days before it occurred to Alain that this was exactly the kind of thing that Roddy might have liked to do to him. But there was no way that Roddy *could* have done it to him. The idea was just paranoia. No, if he was going to salvage anything at all from this situation, he was

going to have to keep his groundless suspicions out of the
way, and keep in favor with Roddy.

Not that Roddy was likely to have the time to so much as
give him a virt-mail at the moment. There certainly hadn't
been any so far. To his astonishment, there *had* been multiple
mails from the Group. A couple of them who lived in the area
had actually come down to the apartment—though he had
been out at the time, and had only his mother's rather grudging
report of this. She hadn't invited them to stay. She thought
they were bad influences on him . . . probably responsible for
his "drug problem."

He sat in his chair and put his face down in his hands,
grateful that no one could see him. *"Drug problem."* As if
he would be so stupid. Oh, he had been as exposed to drugs
as anyone else in his school, but he preferred to run his own
mind, to manage himself, to make things work.

That was worst about this. He had lost control of his own
mind. In front of people.

What if it happened again?

But it couldn't. He wouldn't let it. Not ever.

He laughed hollowly. As if he had been able to stop it when
he originally felt it coming on. That feeling of seeing and
hearing his mouth and his body run away with him, make an
idiot of him, while inside his mind the regular part of him had
hammered futilely on the lining of his brain and shouted, *No,
what are you doing, cut it out—!*

The whole thing reminded him of a horseback riding inci-
dent long ago, when the horse had abruptly broken into a
gallop and he had been able to do nothing but clutch at its
mane and hang on, hang on until it stopped. That awful feeling
of helplessness. Nothing you could do. *Dig in your heels, hang
on harder, yell, scream, it won't make any difference. You're
going to be crazy now.*

He would kill himself before he let that happen again.

The thought shocked him, both by coming out at all, and
by how strongly it came out.

Would I? Would I really do that?

He felt the helplessness again, in memory. The fear . . .

He dared not answer the question. He was too much afraid
of what the answer would be.

For several days Alain actually went to school and paid attention, because the distraction was much preferable to the alternative—hearing the terror and confusion and embarrassment that continued to rage in the back of his head. Some of the guys he hung out with noticed his suddenly quiet look, and started teasing Alain about having possibly fallen in love. He would have punched them all out, except it would have created more trouble than it solved.

And then he got home Thursday night, and worked up the nerve to hook himself into the Net for the first time since his illness, just to check the mail. He didn't know what he was going to find, and was half afraid of what he would. There were more virt-mails from the Group of Seven, particularly a couple from Maj. He ignored them.

But finally, finally he hit the one he had been looking for. From Roddy.

He reached out and poked the mail icon. "Open," he said.

Roddy was sitting somewhere dark, still wearing the tux. *Tell me he hasn't taken it off since the other night,* Alain thought, and smiled slightly, even through the slight sickness in the gut that the thought of the other night produced. It was just like the old Roddy, the one who would cling to any shred of praise.

"Sorry I haven't had time to get this off to you," Roddy said, "but there have been a lot of mails piled up in front of it that needed attention. Tonight's been a pretty lively night. Especially for you."

Tonight? Alain touched the dulled-down mail icon to check the date. It was dated the night of Roddy's opening, a few hours after the event would have finished.

"Continue," Alain said.

Roddy went on. "You'll have worked it out by now, of course. Assuming you've been conscious for a day or so."

Assuming—

"Obviously it wasn't an accident. If you didn't know before, I think you need to know now that people who aren't careful about getting other people to do things for them may eventually suffer the consequences when those things go wrong. And people who think they can routinely mess with other people's minds and get away with it may have nasty

surprises in store for them. Well, that was your first warning . . . and the only one you'll get. Minds can be messed with
in more ways than one . . . as I think you've discovered. And
I would strongly advise you not to discuss this with anyone
else. Virtuality means that anyone can be anywhere, at any
time, without warning. . . .''

And he vanished, or seemed to. The spotlight over his chair
went out, and nothing remained in the darkness but Roddy's
laughter. Finally it faded. . . .

And the message deleted itself.

Alain sat there, frozen with fear at first—that was what
made him most ashamed—and then with growing anger.

The little sonofabitch.

He set me up.

He set me up!!

And I don't even know how—!

That was the source of the fear. *What did he do? How did
he do it?* And almost as bad was the idea that Roddy—always
the slightly disadvantaged one, the one who needed Alain's
help—was suddenly the one who was successful, the one
everyone was paying attention to. And at the apex of that
attention, a moment annoying enough for Alain as it was,
Roddy had managed to make Alain look stupid—or worse,
crazy—in front of half the civilized world, and all the people
who counted—all the people from whom he had ever hoped,
eventually, to get a job.

Well, *that* dream was dead now. Dead too his chances of
ever showing his father that he could find good work simming.
Alain knew that every job interview he ever had would now
contain the thought, spoken or not, *Oh,* this *is the guy who
went around the bend at the Funhouse launch. A liability. Not
for us—*

Revenge. This whole thing had been revenge for Alain suggesting to Roddy that he sabotage Maj's sim, revenge for what
the Group had done to Roddy afterwards. Revenge on *Alain,*
rather than those who deserved it—the Group. They had stood
there and gaped at him when they should have been the ones
on the receiving end of Roddy's wrath.

But how had he done it??

How could you get inside someone's brain, in the virtual world, and make them go nuts?

The fear gripped Alain once more. *He said he could do it again.*

He said—

Somehow Alain wasn't sure. It might be bluff. It would suit Roddy well to have him sitting around frozen, afraid to do anything.

But what if it's not a bluff?

Alain sat there and swallowed. Swallowed again, convulsively.

Well, even if it is . . .

I can't let him get away with this.

Revenge.

Alain frowned. *He wants revenge? I'm sure I can accommodate him.*

I have a few sources of my own that have some clout. If Roddy's screwing around with people's minds in the virtual world, there's one bunch of people who're going to be real pleased to find out about it. They'll come down on him like a ton of bricks. They'll chuck him in a cell and contract the door, and he'll never be seen again.

They'll take care of him good.

Net Force . . .

Alain gestured his address book to him, out of the darkness, and went through it, looking for Rachel Halloran's code.

The same afternoon, Roddy L'Officier was in the back of a private limo, going to a meeting. He could hardly believe it. He couldn't remember when he had last had the money to ride in a cab, let alone a private stretch limo . . . and he hadn't even paid for this one. "We'll send a car," they'd said, the people on the other end—after they had asked for the privilege of seeing him personally. The privilege!

Roddy kept finding himself swallowing and surreptitiously wiping his palms on his pants, and his mouth was too dry for him to do much more than exchange a couple of inane pleasantries with the car's suave and cheerful driver. The idea kept recurring that this was all some kind of crazy dream. . . . But Roddy didn't dare let himself believe that. It would hurt too much, and the thought of the look on his mother's face, triumphant, vindicated, when it all turned out to be a hoax and came to an end, would be too much to bear.

The skeptical look had been on her face even this morning, even after the last couple of days. On the morning of the Funhouse opening, while fielding the initial calls from the media, his mother had been scathing. She'd thought Roddy was getting some of his "weird simming friends" to play tricks on her, and she'd bawled him out once or twice.

Then the opening happened, and the next morning, while Roddy was still in bed trying to recover, the link just wouldn't stop sounding. His mother refused to use visual to answer it—she never used visual until after noon, something she said was to do with "privacy," but though Roddy thought had more to do with how long it took her to get her face made up the way she liked—and when *The New York Times* called the house, she hollered at the pickup, "I don't want a subscription, now go away!"

The reporter had to call her back three times to get her to understand that he didn't want to sell her a subscription. He wanted to interview her son. She didn't believe him then either. But when the man turned up on her doorstep with *Times* ID and a photographer . . . her manner changed. Shortly after that, CNN turned up, and she actually let them in with only minimal makeup on, and started acting the gracious hostess and referring to her "dear son Rod."

Roddy had to smile, but he'd kept to himself what he thought of her posturing (and the way it stopped after the CNN crew left). At this point, publicity was going to be important, and he intended to make sure all of it was good. For one thing, the school authorities were likely enough to turn up soon, demanding to know why he wasn't attending again—and he intended to have some kind of contract signed, in a hurry, that would mean enough money for private teaching for the rest of his minority. No more having to sit in a public school with the deadheads, no more of their jeers at his clothes and his looks . . .

. . . if this worked.

He rubbed his hands on his pants again, and considered that the clothes at least were handled for the moment. Even in just a day he'd scored enough from the initial rush of checkbook journalism surrounding the opening of the Funhouse for him to put away money for a rainy day. And yesterday, when the call had come in from the EnTastics people, he had gone out and for the first time dared to buy himself some of the neat clothes he'd wanted for so long, the kind of things that he was going to need to do business with the business people.

Today, for the first time, he looked like a hot young executive—no longer threadbare, no longer in the second-hand stuff that was all his mom was able to afford on her pitiful salary. It was sweet, to someone for whom one had long been the "loneliest number," someone trapped in an isolation that had become a matter of habit. For a little while, at least, he would be able to afford aircabs and eating out. It was temporary, of course. He knew the initial flush of money would eventually run out, and he was managing it with some care.

He rubbed his palms dry one more time, squirming slightly. The limo was coming down toward the private garage beneath a building in one of the large exclusive upper-level industrial parks near Falls Church. Up above Roddy spread a huge expanse of glass and steel buildings, the EnTastics main East Coast facility: a place that Roddy had never dreamed he would see the inside of in his life. He swallowed while the limo's engines screamed a little louder as the walls reflected the noise inward just before stopping.

Thunk—and almost before he had time to draw breath, someone had slapped the outside release for the door, and a stunning young woman smiled at him and said, "Mr. L'Officier? I'm Stella Hansen. The directors are waiting to meet you. . . ."

She led him, smiling and chatting, into a glass shelter near the limo, into an elevator in the shelter, and up to the penthouse. When the door opened again, Roddy found himself looking out into what appeared to be about twenty acres of open floor space, studded with mini-offices, computer installations, virtual seats and tanks and "implant pockets." And hurrying toward the elevator, actually hurrying, were the joint directors of EnTastics, Elberts and Robyns.

Most people would have known them immediately from the commercials, which had made them as famous as Ben and

Jerry had been in an earlier decade: Joss, tall and thin, with his hair thinning slightly on top, a young man with a dry, funny smile and quick eyes: and Erin, shorter, rounder, and with more hair than Joss, but just as young, and with a grin closely allied to his in wickedness, suddenness, and the ease with which it appeared. They had become more or less the Laurel and Hardy of modern virtual "game" computing, the kind of teenage millionaires who were now role models and icons for Roddy's generation—starting their company in Joss's little sister's bedroom, and winding up (for the moment) here.

Roddy shook their hands, glad that he'd managed to wipe his hand one more time before he got out of the elevator. He hardly knew what to say to them.

It didn't matter. "Great playroom," Joss said, and Erin said, "Yeah, his tongue's been hanging out for the better part of two days; you should have seen him when he fell into the diamond cave and couldn't get out," Erin said, and Joss said, "Come on, take a look at what we're working on—"

And they were off across the huge acreage of floor, talking a mile a minute, with Roddy in tow. Roddy was dazed at first by the surroundings and the company. He managed to answer Joss's and Erin's questions, at least, and he had the manners to ooh and aah at some of the new developments they showed him, like the improved Black Tank.

Not that he wouldn't have anyway. As they showed him around the development "shop floor" of EnTastics, Roddy was repeatedly consumed by that particular delighted envy peculiar to the inventive mind which hasn't thought of something first, but sees it executed somewhere else, and knows it *could* have thought of it.

Slowly, though, it began to sink in that Erin and Joss were not being nice to him because they merely wanted to get their hands on his playroom technology or techniques, but because they genuinely saw him as one of their own kind, one of them. Roddy was utterly astonished. Again and again Roddy would sneak a look at one or the other of them to try to catch the covert look, the sly expression that would make plain that it was all a joke, a ploy. But the look was never there. Joss and Erin meant it. They asked Roddy for his opinion as if it mattered. They were seriously interested in his reactions to their equipment and several of their own virtual playrooms—in one case Roddy, turning at the right moment, caught Joss actually holding his breath to see what Roddy thought.

It made all the difference in the world to him. Slowly Roddy started to gather courage, found himself able to speak a sentence or so without being spoken to first and without sounding like an utter geek. He found that he could grin, even laugh out loud without it sounding artificial and terrified. By the end of the afternoon Roddy was making jokes with the assumption that Joss and Erin would laugh, and no longer grinning with relief when they did, but with plain enjoyment. And he was suggesting ways for them to improve some of the scenarios that they showed him—an act of sheer mad bravado he would have been incapable of just three hours before. But in three hours, everything had turned around. The dream was a reality. This was his world, the place where he was meant to be. He was home at last.

Joss and Erin had a previous engagement for dinner, a fact that made them groan repeatedly. They wanted to continue the conversation . . . but it would have to wait. At last they reluctantly took Roddy back down to the garage, where the private limo was waiting, along with one of their corporate ones. They shook Roddy's hand (which was now dry without having to be wiped), and saw him off before heading off themselves.

Roddy sat there in the car, staring at the business cards that Erin and Joss had given him. He had come away from EnTastics with their private e-mail addresses . . . and much more: with the sense that he really had made it, that he really was hot stuff. That, whatever else this might be, it wasn't a dream. The private limousine had a virt hookup, which he had been too nervous to use on the way in to EnTastics. Now, on the way home, Roddy used it again to check his mail, and found numerous messages waiting for him, inviting him to meetings. Yesterday they would have terrified him. Today, though, he had had a five-hour meeting with Joss and Erin. And after that, there was nothing left to be scared of. . . .

In fact, if today was anything to go by, shortly Roddy would be signing on one or another of the big companies that were already sniffing around the Funhouse, looking for ways to co-opt his talent. All these meetings would give Roddy the chance to let it be known that he could be co-opted, all right, for a deal with the right number of zeroes after it. He would have a lot of things to do . . . and no more time for most aspects of his old life. Including the poor pathetic Group of Seven. Roddy wouldn't need some of the more clandestine features he had built into the Funhouse. He could use that space for more Funhouse business.

Yes, things were definitely looking up. But what mattered much more—so much that he didn't dare say it out loud—was that, at last, at long last he was the important one. Nobody was looking at Roddy and thinking secretly, *He's useless, he's lazy, he'll never come to anything.* No one was saying any of the things he was used to hearing at home, over and over. He would show the business cards to his mother, and finally she would have to admit that he had made good. From that quarter, finally, there would be some silence . . . and from everywhere else, the sound of applause.

Late the next day, a chime sounded softly in a house in a beachfront community on the Jersey Shore. The house was big and open and airy, full of clean, simple canvas and wicker furniture, its windows open to the sea air and the thin white curtains blowing into the living room, stirred by the breeze from the beach. It looked like a house waiting for the photographers from *Architectural Digest*: a little too orderly, a little too clean for people to actually live there.

The chime sounded again, and a woman walked into the room and sighed, putting down a glass of white wine. She was dressed simply in a floaty ecru-colored summer dress that would have been more fashionable in the late twentieth century, it being the kind of twisted cotton gauze that was popular for summer wear then. Otherwise, there was nothing particularly unusual about her. She was pretty, though in a severe way more reminiscent of an old Greek statue than of any of the models who appeared in the fashion media these days. Long dark hair spilled down her back, tied in an informal ponytail. This fell forward over her shoulder as she leaned over the computer box in the front room to see what the source of the chime was.

"Oh, really," she said softly after a moment. She turned to line up her implant with the "black box" sitting at the end of the wicker couch. "Wake up."

The living room faded to a nondescript silvery haze. "Set three," the woman said.

All around her, the haze changed to a much-subdivided and compartmented office done in shades of gray. Computers were scattered everywhere, while here and there people sat in chairs with their implants lined up. In one spot or another, streams of data scrolled down through the air. Out the windows of the office, an alert viewer would have made out a view of the landscape just outside Quantico, with the blue ribbon of the Potomac just visible past the trees in the distance.

The woman's dress was now a much more reserved navy and charcoal jacket-and-pants combination with a plain white Oxford-cloth shirt underneath it, and a subdued scarf. A holographic photo ID hung from the jacket pocket.

"Net Force," she said. "Halloran."

After a moment she found herself looking at Alain Thurston, one of her younger contacts. "Alain," she said, schooling herself to look surprised, "thanks for calling again. I got your message from yesterday, but I wasn't free to handle it until I got back to my desk a little while ago. How are you? Haven't heard from you in a while."

"I've been better," Alain said. There was something about his tone of voice that brought her to a slightly higher state of alertness than she was willing to manifest, to this kid at least.

"Why? What's the problem?"

"I just got out of the hospital."

"Nothing serious, I hope." She looked up for a moment, and reached off to take a paper file folder that someone out of frame "handed" her.

"Meningitis."

"My gosh, where did you pick that up? Are you okay?"

"I'm all right now, Rachel. But I picked it up on the Net."

She looked at him with understandable skepticism. "From someone you met on the Net, you mean."

"Yes, but not the way you mean," Thurston said. His normally bland and suave young face looked angry. "I mean, someone gave me something contagious, on the Net—and he did it on purpose.''

"That's impossible," she said. "Or—it *should* be impossible."

"Well," Thurston said, "somebody forgot to tell *this* guy it's impossible. He's found a way to do it."

The story that Alain spun her went on for the better part of half an hour, with many bizarre excursions that were supposed to explain what was unquestionably a very complex and toxic relationship between Alain and someone named Roddy L'Officier. Rachel let him tell the story without too much in the way of interruption, mostly because she had heard the L'Officier name recently. There had been a spectacular launch of a virtual "playroom"—much too big for the term, really—and a lot of people had been very impressed by the technology, or rather the new and inventive implementation of the present technology, that had been implied by the "Funhouse."

Rachel listened patiently to Alain's tale of grievance and revenge, nodding in all the right places and looking interested. Normally she wouldn't have wasted her time—these younger marks were almost without exception pitifully self-centered, and would talk the sun out of the sky and your patience into rags if you let them. But this. *Meningitis.*

"I'd like to see the notes from the hospital," she said after a while. "I take it they sent copies for addition to your personal file, the normal stuff that goes to the insurance company and so forth."

"Oh, yeah," Alain said, "they sent all that stuff to my dad. Not that he's interested."

"Why on earth wouldn't he be interested?"

"He doesn't believe it was meningitis. He's sure I was doing drugs or something."

Rachel blinked at that. She knew that Alain's relationship with his father was less than perfect, but this was interesting—possibly something that could be played on to good effect later. "Well, that seems a little far-fetched, knowing you," she said. "Alain, I would like to see those records. If I can get you to forward them to me—"

"No problem."

"Because if this is indeed something that he managed to

give you via the Net—'' She shook her head. "That would
be a terrible threat. Something that would have to be stopped
immediately. My God, the ramifications—''

"Yeah," Alain said, and his eyes gleamed. "I imagine
Roddy wouldn't do too well out of it.''

"He might get a break if he cooperated with us," Rachel
said, "but—''

Alain shook his head with a certain look of satisfaction.
"No way," he said, "absolutely no way will he cooperate
with anybody. He's riding high at the moment." He subsided
slightly. "And besides, there's no proof. The message he sent
me didn't come right out and say anything—and even that he
sent in self-erase format.''

Rachel shook her head impatiently. "Come on, Alain," she
said. "We've known each other for a while now. You're a
smart kid, too smart to lie to me, and certainly too smart to
just make something like this up on the off chance that it'll
get someone in trouble. Especially when your later career
might depend on it.''

She gave him Knowing Smile #2, the slightly understated
one. He showed a weak smile in response. "So," Rachel said.
"If I can substantiate this—then I'd say your 'friend' Roddy
is going to have a lot to answer for. Obviously it's going to
take me a little time to look into this. Will you get me those
records, and then leave the matter with me?''

"Sure. I'll mail them over to you this morning.''

"If he really *has* found out how to manage this, and you
turn out to be the one who's caught him out at it—we're going
to have a lot to thank you for.''

"Well, I don't want this to happen to anyone else . . . that's
all.''

"Of course not. Alain, I think you've done the right thing
bringing this to me. Leave it with me—I'll get back to you as
soon as I know something concrete. And thanks again.''

"Uh, yeah. Thanks, Rachel—a lot.''

He was gone.

She stood up straight, sighed, and said to the computer, "Go
to sleep.''

Virtuality vanished. The beach house came back, and the

summer dress, and the glass of white wine sitting on the low table nearby.

Rachel Halloran—not that that was her real name, of course—sat down in the big comfy chair by the table, reached out for the white wine, and began to think hard.

"I just don't want this to happen to anyone else." That made her chuckle out loud.

What transparent bullshit. He hates this other kid's guts, and he wants to see him put away.

She raised her eyebrows, and sipped at the wine. *Not that I'd blame him. If someone tried the same trick with me, I'd want to tie their guts to a tree and chase them around it.*

If the trick was for real. And if it is . . .

She thought for a few minutes, considering what would be the best way to proceed. She did not want to lose Alain as a potential tool, though that might have to happen. Her employers tended to get very cranky about the possibility of anyone revealing what lines of inquiry their operatives had been pursuing, especially when it had cost so much time and trouble to set this whole operation up—most particularly the apparently valid Net Force IDs and e-mail addresses, which had taken vast amounts of money and technical expertise to finagle, and without which the whole operation would never have gotten off the ground. All it would take was one wrong word getting out to the genuine Net Force, which had already made their work hard enough with its vigilance, and the whole wide-flung intelligence-exploitation operation would come apart . . . almost certainly with terminal results for the operative closest to the leak.

But on the other side of the argument, this particular line of inquiry could be worth a lot to the op who tracked the proper instrumentality down. If it worked, if it worked *repeatedly,* and reliably—

Virtual communicability.

Among covert intelligence organizations the world over, and overt ones as well, virtual or "remote" communicability— the ability to infect someone from a distance, tracelessly, with a disease—was the Holy Grail. Any disease would do, to start with. Even being able to give people the common cold over the Net would be a stunt that could bring its inventor millions—if only from the people who sold cold medicines. By the time the vector was found and stopped, the drug companies would have made back their investment a hundredfold.

But serious diseases—*those* were every covert operation group's dream. Terrorists would pay anything for the ability to inflict terminal diseases on their enemies from a distance, especially secretly: the virtual equivalent of the letter bomb. Nations at war would leap at the chance to kill their enemies without having to take the field themselves or get their expensive military hardware blown up. There were hundreds, thousands of possibilities.

The problem was the mind-body barrier. There was no way to cross it. The virtual world was trapped on the other side of a wall that it could not pierce, and no one had found even an inkling, as yet, of how to do it. All that was needed was one tiny hint—one little chink in the wall—and then the human mind and body would no longer be safe or distinct from virtual phenomena.

It had to be said that there were those even among the most opportunistic intelligence communities who had been resisting research or development into this area. They argued that to break down that barrier between physical reality, at least as it involved the human body, and the nonphysical realities like the Net, could possibly cause the collapse of civilization itself—a massive "meltdown" in which no one would any longer be able to tell the difference between the genuine physical realities played out in diplomacy and battles across the face of the planet, and the constructed realities that were of much less value by the nature of their construction. Take away the difference between "real life" and "virtual life," these people argued, and soon neither would mean more than the other—a state that kings and presidents and superpowers would shortly find untenable. Some said that such a breakdown would cause the last world war, in which the merely physical powers attempted to assert their superiority over the virtual ones. And there would be no winners of such a war, and possibly no survivors.

Rachel personally found those concerns a little on the abstruse side. She suspected that human beings would find a way to survive, no matter what was being done to them. At least,

ONE IS THE LONELIEST NUMBER

some of them would . . . the winners, in other words. She free-lanced for various organizations, all of whom were concerned about being on the winning side, sooner or later, in any one of a number of conflicts and arenas. One of the arenas was weaponry. And virtual communicability would be a weapon and a half.

If she could confirm its existence . . . and get hold of the technique. Once tested, if it worked, she could move this beach house to Grand Cayman and retire. But there would be a fair amount of work to do first. She would have to readopt her "Net Force" persona—a perfect cover for the kind of work she was involved in—and do a little snooping, then confront this Roddy, this skewed young genius, and throw the fear of God into him.

Virtual anthrax, she thought. *Virtual cholera. Virtual rabies.*

What a concept. . . .

Rachel sat in the comfy chair for a few moments more, then got up and went into the back room to do a little research, and make some calls.

7

Two days later, Roddy L'Officier was walking down a street in Bethesda, Maryland, making his way confidently to yet another of the business meetings with which his days had been full since the opening of the Funhouse. The address of his meeting was in one of the more affluent office building complexes, supposedly one of the places where a lot of the more discreet government agencies had offices—an area mostly consisting of architecturally ambitious high-rises slick with glass and recessed night lighting.

The building in question was some kind of mixed-business site, not owned by one company, or seeming not to be: set back from the road, with IR cameras looking at the front accesses, and raked-sand gardens adorning both sides of the path to the front doors. Roddy looked casually at the gardens as he headed for the doors. *Japanese money?* he thought. *Or maybe Singapore* . . . They were all hot for increased implementation of the virtual technologies, with their ever-expanding populations and ever-decreasing space to work with. Roddy had heard stories that there were parts of Japan now where, if you didn't make enough money to afford something better, your "house" was about twice the size of a coffin, and everything in it was virtual except waste disposal . . . and they were working on that. *Not my problem,* Roddy thought. *But let's see what they're after.* . . .

The company whose executive he was meeting with was

called Sixth Circle Productions: apparently another entertainment production group that farmed virtual entertainments of various kinds out to the major providers. The lady had a direct way about her, a nice smile, and the way she had dressed in the virt-mails they'd exchanged suggested serious money in the background—all Hermés, from the jacket and skirt right down to the single discreet white enamel bangle. Roddy had become something of a connoisseur of the way his business connections dressed, and he was enjoying that too. In the old days he hated looking at people's nice clothes, as they always reminded him of how few of them he had of his own, how he had to scrimp and save what little money his mom gave him to afford the new clothes that were the only ones he allowed himself to be seen in. It had been one of the reasons why he didn't get out much, except virtually. But now all that had changed. . . .

He walked in, and gave the smiling receptionist his name and the name of the lady he had come to see. "Ninth floor," said the receptionist, and Roddy got into the elevator and rode up sedately, only once checking the set of his collar in the bronze-mirror finish of the elevator doors.

They opened, and he stepped out into a plushly carpeted space done in dark woods and autumn colors. Out of a nearby door immediately came the executive he had come to meet. "Mr. L'Officier," she said, and shook his hand genially, "glad you could find time to work us in today."

"Ms. Halloran," Roddy said, "my pleasure."

"Will you come this way?"

They stepped into her office, and she shut the door behind them.

"Can I get you something before we start?" she asked.

"Tea would be nice," Roddy said.

"Michael," she said to the air, "tea for Mr. L'Officier, please. How do you take it?"

"Two sugars."

"Fine. The usual for me, Michael. Please, Mr. L'Officier, sit down and make yourself comfortable."

"Please," he said, sinking down into the handsome hide chair across from her desk. "Call me Roddy."

"Thank you, Roddy. Please call me Rachel. I'm glad you

were able to come in, because my company is very excited about some of the technologies implicit in your Funhouse development. We're interested in the possibility of licensing some of the more accessible options—''

It started out that way, as so many of the other interviews had, and at first Roddy was only half listening. He was busy assessing the look and feel of the office (affluent: Over by the door, acting as the doorstop, was a piece of rough marrowfat jade the size of his head) and its occupant (very smooth, very cool indeed; she would have been intimidating, had Roddy not had something that she wanted) and her support personnel (the sharply but expensively dressed young man who materialized with the tea, put it deferentially in front of Roddy, and vanished again).

What made it all even more terrific was that, as they started to discuss the technical details, Rachel was plainly completely familiar with the kinds of things he was doing—or rather, with the technologies they were based on. Her own straightforward pleasure in what she apparently saw as his extreme cleverness was kind of endearing too. Some of these people would sit there with a poker face and not let on what they thought about anything you were doing, except that they hated your guts for thinking of it first, and wanted a piece of it while giving you as little back for the privilege as possible.

That being the case, Roddy had been treating most of these meetings with considerable caution, while still enjoying them. But this one went further into enjoyment than usual—if this lady was anything to go by, the firm had some very intelligent and congenial people in it—and he was slowly beginning to consider varying his usual response, which was to say ''no'' to everybody, or at least to leave them with the feeling that they would need to improve their original offers a lot before he would be ready to start saying ''yes.'' Rachel started suggesting such innovative uses of Roddy's implementations of sim technology that it all started feeling a lot more like fun, and a lot less like business.

She wanted to know a fair amount about how he had originally gotten started. ''Nothing secret now!'' she said with a laugh, ''Just the generalities.'' And it was so refreshing to hear someone saying that they didn't *want* to hear your secrets that he wound up telling her more than he intended to about his basic programming structures. Not enough to use, of course, but she was so smart about the implications that she got up a couple times and walked around the room practically waving her arms, and laughing from the sheer pleasure at what Roddy had managed to pull off. So much content in such a small space, and the elegance of it . . .

Roddy was impressed that anyone could understand the source of his greatest pleasure in simming—that very elegance, that maximization of the resources when you only had a little money and had to make everything count. It wasn't anything like the products of some of the firms he knew who were big in the simming business, or even people working freelance, like the group he'd been involved with but had to leave because they were too hung up on money and space, and not enough on the quality of the sim and the effect you produced.

"Oh, *tell* me about it," Rachel said, rolling her eyes slightly. And then she told him about one of the companies she had worked with before breaking loose to come here, and when she was done, Roddy regaled her with tales of the Group of Seven, who purported to want to do quality simming, but who were actually all about head games and ego massage, about the demand for unwarranted praise, and about being bad losers when they didn't get it. In fact there had been a little joke played on one of them at the launch.

"They didn't actually show up there, did they?" Rachel looked amused and surprised. "But they said they weren't going to have anything more to do with you!"

"I know," Roddy said, "but they sneaked in. I didn't mind it from most of them, it was kind of a backwards compliment, but one of them in particular, this guy who had been pretending to be my friend and confidant and was actually out to steal whatever he could—well, when he showed up . . ."

Roddy paused, ever so briefly thinking, *Should I?* Rachel's eyes were glinting with good-natured amusement, and she put her eyebrows up in anticipation of what he was going to say next. "Well," Roddy said, "I surprised him a little. Left him a little present in the playroom's code . . . and left him hors de combat.'' He chuckled. ''Next time he'll wait for a formal invitation.''

''But Roddy, that's *assault*,'' Rachel said, still amused. ''Not that you didn't have provocation.''

''Yeah, well,'' Roddy said. ''After what he did to me—''

''But provocation isn't a mitigating factor,'' Rachel said. Was there something slightly different about her smile now? ''Alain Thurston wound up in the hospital with meningitis. Purposely infecting someone with a potentially fatal disease is classed as aggravated assault under state and Federal statutes.''

Roddy opened his mouth, closed it again. ''But—''

Rachel reached inside her jacket, pulled out a small wallet-sized slip-case, flipped it open, and pushed it across the desk to Roddy. He looked at it, and the sweat broke out all over him on the spot.

Net Force!

''I think we have a problem here,'' Rachel said softly.

Roddy took in the ID. He had heard of them before, these unfakeable identifications, but he had never seen one before—and never thought he would. The holograms, the virtual-experience chip, they were all there.

''Go on,'' Rachel said. ''You have a right to check it.''

Roddy reached out a tentative hand and touched the virt-chip with it. Immediately his vision clouded over, and the Net Force logo, repeated many times as a background, appeared in the air before him, with Rachel's face, rotating, in front of it. Various signatures besides Rachel's appeared at the bottom of the representation, one of them saying, in a very clean and precise hand, *J. GRIDLEY*.

Roddy gulped, turned in his seat, and looked over his shoulder.

''Not a chance,'' Rachel said with some compassion. ''You would never make it as far as the elevator.''

''You tricked me into—''

''Did I?'' Rachel said. ''Let's be honest about this at least. You were eager to tell me. You've been burning to tell *somebody*. You were actually going to tell Alain, but stopped just short of incriminating yourself. Smart . . . but not smart enough.'' She shook her head.

Roddy was shaking all over now, though he was trying to

control it. "What are—" he said, and had to stop, because
his mouth was suddenly too dry to speak. "What are you
going to do?"

Rachel sat back in her chair and studied him. After a very
long pause, she said, "That depends on you."

Roddy was about to shout, *What do you mean, you're saying I've committed a crime, get on with it and arrest me!* But
some more survival-oriented part of his brain got control of
his mouth and held it still.

She looked at him.

"Yes," she said, and was silent for a moment more.
"Waste," she said at last, "waste is a sad thing. We try to
prevent it, when we can. I would dislike having to call—say,
your mother—and explain to her how your talent had been
wasted because of a single misstep."

Oh, God, his mother. The very thought held him as still as
a bird that had suddenly found itself staring at a rattlesnake.

"So," Rachel said, "let's talk a little about what you did."

"It's hard to explain," Roddy said, terrified.

"I bet it is," Rachel said, "when you're uncertain about
your status. Let's be clear about your status, so that we can
get on with things. You've admitted virtual assault on an innocent party to a Net Force operative. There's no possible
excuse of self-defense or insanity or flight or *desperandum* or
any of the usual outs. Your service provider, if we ask them,
will be only too glad to turn over to us everything that pertains
to your workspace. We will then take it apart, atom by atom
of solid storage, until we find out what you did and how you
did it. It might take us months . . . years. *You,* of course, will
be in a Federal correctional facility. Interstate felony assault
with intent, endangering the public, various other charges.
You're old enough to be charged as an adult in your home
state. I think you would find your circumstances . . . uncomfortable."

Roddy sat there and shook.

"Waste," Rachel said, folding her hands. "Waste of time.
I dislike that too. Let me say two words to you: *parallel development.*"

Roddy blinked.

"It's one of those strange things we don't fully understand," Rachel said, "a subsection of chaos theory. It came to the scientific community's attention about a hundred years ago. Some monkeys on an isolated Pacific island discovered after they'd dug up the local wild tubers, a kind of sweet potato, that washing the potatoes in the sea afterwards made them more palatable. Not very interesting . . . until scientists studying Pacific simians got together and compared notes, and found that all over the Pacific, within a few months of that innovation, *all* the monkeys were washing their sweet potatoes. How did the word get around? Hardly by virt-mail."

Rachel sat back again and turned the white bangle on her wrist around a few times slowly. "Something unusual and new that happens suddenly in one place is likely to happen suddenly in many other places shortly thereafter," she said. "The odds are *much* better than even. So . . . if *you've* found a technique by which people can somehow be infected with diseases over the Net, then the odds are high, significantly so, that someone else will work out how to do it within months . . . maybe weeks."

Rachel leaned forward over the desk, looked Roddy directly in the eyes, and spoke intensely. "I want that jump on the competition. Do you understand me? *I want to be ahead of the bad guys on this one.* You've done enough work on the subject to give someone a little infection. Minor, not much more trouble than a cold, not really, from the medical side: nasty to start with, easy enough to cure. The people who make their livings by killing other people won't stop with that kind of thing. The sicknesses they virt-mail people will be deadly. They could bring the planet screeching to a halt . . . or bring civilization to an end."

Roddy stopped shaking . . . mostly because of shock. This was definitely not an aspect of the situation he had considered. He *liked* civilization.

"You're in trouble," Rachel said. "I'm offering you a way to walk out of this one . . . and maybe even come out a hero. Help us work out what you did. Take us into your code, run us through it, show us how you did the trick. Show us the defenses against it. And more than that, take it further. Make it *worse*. It's a weapon? Good, then finish building it. When the other monkeys try this technique on the good guys for the

irst time, virtual or live, I want to unleash on them in response
a variant on the theme so deadly that they'll *never* dare mess
with this technology again. They'll drop it—like a hot po-
ato''—she smiled, ever so briefly—''and never again try to
venture down this particular road.''

Roddy swallowed, swallowed again, now that he was able
o. ''And afterwards,'' he said. ''What happens to me?''

Rachel leaned back, shrugged. ''If you get the job done
right,'' she said, ''then naturally that would count as mitigat-
ng circumstances. And after that . . . well, we don't forget our
own.'' The smile was cool. ''Every company can use a few
'reverse assets.' Hackers who grow up and get involved with
protecting the systems they used to try to break. They know
all the secrets. They're valuable. They look at the present systems and work to patch up holes in them before the holes
happen . . . learn to prevent the breaches that would otherwise
cripple whole industries. It's good work. Worth doing.''

She looked at him with compassion again. ''You made a
mistake,'' Rachel said. ''Got angry, didn't think a course of
action through. It happens. Fortunately . . . very fortunately for
you . . . you're in a position where you can atone for that mistake.''

She fell silent, and sat looking quietly at him.

Roddy stared at the Net Force ID sitting on the desk between them. He stared at it for a long time . . . and thought of
his mother.

''Okay,'' he said at last. ''What do you want to know
first?''

Roddy stood in the darkness, waiting. He was shaking again,
without good reason.

Well, he *had* good reason. . . .

Net Force. The long arm of the law . . . with its hand
wrapped around his throat, and squeezing. He had thought that
he would be wily, would be cool, in the face of any opposition
to what he was doing. Now he knew the truth, and it was
bitter to him. The more bitter because there was nowhere to
run from it, no fantasy left in which he could hide.

And besides that . . . in its way, even worse than that . . . the
phone calls had stopped.

His mother had at first claimed to be relieved by this, but that hadn't lasted. Within a day or so she was angry, convinced that Roddy had somehow offended someone, or messed something up. She was close enough to the truth in this regard that, for those few days that followed, she had nearly gotten back again the slightly cowed son that she was used to—the one who didn't talk back, didn't argue. He wondered who had put the word out about him that he was no good to talk to anymore.

He could guess.

His mother wouldn't stop going on about "the changes in their lives." Whenever he was non-virtual, she was constantly on his case, nagging and complaining: bitching about the news people, bitching about them suddenly not being there anymore, annoyed that everyone was paying attention to her son, annoyed that they had stopped. Roddy didn't argue the point with her, just let her talk. He had more important things to think about. He was spending almost all of his time in the Net, working for his life.

Many of the techniques Roddy was now evolving, at breakneck speed, were based on conjectures about which he had only made some random notes in the previous few months. Now, suddenly, they had to become full-fledged subroutines . . . and they were now becoming such: so quickly, in some cases, that Roddy was frightened. With the relationships among the neurotransmitter chemicals, in particular, he was winging it. But he had found that desperation was a powerful incentive to getting things done that he didn't normally think were possible. It was nearly as useful a spur as rage, though not nearly as enjoyable.

Now he stood in the dark and looked at the huge cubical array of his Caldera program, shimmering there, all straight lines, logical and solid. Or it *should* have looked solid. Right now, because of its newness, the whole thing looked desperately jury-rigged and tentative to Roddy. He wasn't used to his programming looking that way. He didn't like it. Normally he had days to get used to the structure after a set of changes, to see it "settle" in his mind and seem reliable again. Now though, he had made hundreds of changes in mere hours . .

d it all looked to him like a structure that might come apart
ywhere, without warning.

It had better not, though. He had no desire to wind up in
il . . . or worse.

In the darkness he heard sound—footsteps—and turned to-
ard them. Roddy had had no choice but to give Rachel his
asswords. Now she came strolling along across the huge
npty space in which Roddy kept his programming, looking
ound her and up at the Caldera structure as she came, like
restrained and interested tourist. He would have preferred to
age this meeting in the Hall of the Mountain King, with his
aves creeping and cringing around the way he crept and
inged around his mother, but he doubted Rachel would have
opreciated the humor.

Probably not. Her face was set as she came up to him, and
gain Roddy got the feeling that it would be very unwise to
tempt anything funny with her, either funny-clever or funny-
ıha.

"Roddy," she said, "good morning. Is this it?"

"This is it," he said.

"Impressive," she said, looking up. "Quite a structure.
ow long did it take you to build this up?"

"A couple of months." It had taken more time, of course,
uch more, but he'd never admit it to this woman.

She nodded, her face unrevealing. "But not the new parts."

"I've been busy since we talked last. . . ."

"I bet you have. So tell me what the new parts of this
ructure do exactly."

Her voice was impatient. Roddy shook his head at the hope-
essness of doing something like that simply or quickly, and
: the unfairness of having to try, when so much of the beauty
f the work was in the detail. "They build a mirror of your
ody on a molecular level," Roddy said. "The mirror runs in
irtuality, in exact sync with the original. That's why there's
o much memory here." He waved a hand at the pertinent
arts of the program structure, which glowed golden in re-
ponse: a stutter of lines and interwoven strands and ropes of
ght through the greater program structure. "Or rather, the
ıbroutine mirrors *parts* of your body—even I can't fit enough
ıemory in here to handle all the information that a whole

body implies. It mirrors the nervous system mostly, and th
brain. Even that takes a lot of memory. The energy states i
the atoms and molecules of the brain and nervous system kee
changing, and the mirror has to change with them.''

"So," Rachel said, "your physical body—*responds* to th
mirror?''

"It gets confused," Roddy said. "It starts losing its sens
of which system is real, because there's communication be
tween the real body and the virtual one, and there's no tim
difference between them—or such a little one, microsecond
worth, that a system running on something as slow as bic
electricity doesn't notice. There are no echoes. The two sys
tems become identified with one another. Then when yo
change the virtual one—''

"The real one changes too," Rachel said very quietly.

"That's right," Roddy said. "When that happens, then yo
start laying in instructions. You have the brain and the pitu
tary and pineal glands and so on, all the sources of messenge
chemicals, tell the liver and the lymphatic system to start man
ufacturing certain proteins and protein fragments out of th
raw materials available in the body—the basic amino acid
that everyone gets in their food. And when those proteins ar
available, you tell the spleen and liver and so on to store c
manipulate the chemicals in certain specific ways.''

" 'Logic bombs,' " Rachel said. "But biological ones."

"More or less. There's all kinds of information you ca
program into the body, especially in durable structures like fa
cells, if your 'elements of code' are small enough. Like, yo
can tell the body to fail to respond to certain organisms whe
they come along with a specific marking on them. The im
mune system just *ignores* those organisms, even though it'
working fine. No amount of artificial stimulation of the im
mune system would make any difference to that particular in
fection. It just wouldn't be able to 'see' it. And you could te
it *when* not to see it. The body has its own clocks, several c
them that can be plotted against each other to determine du
ration. You could tell someone to get sick in a week, or
year, or ten years, when the right bug came along, and they'
do it. They might even be carrying the right bug with the

for all that time, and nothing would happen until you'd told it to."

Roddy couldn't help starting to smile a little now. The programming to manage this particular piece of business had been deadly difficult, but he'd managed it, and he was proud. This was stuff that he'd be able to put to good use in the Funhouse later on, when all this blew over.

Rachel just nodded. "Okay," she said, "I follow you so far. But it sounds like you're telling me that you'll need a non-virtual part of this 'syndrome' to make it work best. A genuine infectious agent of some kind."

"Bacteria are easiest," Roddy said. "They're not as interesting as viruses are these days. Everyone sort of takes them for granted. And they're hardier than viruses, some ways. You can give them to your target in food or water, or in the air as a spray—however you like, because if you've done it right, that bacterium can't do any harm to anybody but the person it's tailored for. It gets into their body, and the chemical instructions planted in the body 'recognize' it and act in whatever way you've told them to. The body 'fails to react,' say— and comes down with a bad infection that won't respond to immunostimulation. You'd probably want to use a strain that's resistant to antibiotics—"

"Or one that no antibiotic could stop to begin with," Rachel said, looking thoughtful.

"TB, or *Neopasteurella,* something like that," Roddy said. "Yeah. The bad guys wouldn't like *that* much. . . ."

"No," Rachel said, "I dare say they won't. . . ."

"But the person gets sick and goes into the hospital, and nothing the doctors can do will stop what's wrong with him," Roddy said. "They won't even think there's an immune system problem, I bet, because the system will be *working* . . . just not on this one bug. By the time anyone figures out what's going on . . . if they ever do—"

"The target would be dead," Rachel said.

Roddy nodded.

Rachel was quiet for a long time. "All right," she said at last. "When can we start testing?"

"Uh . . . It's not quite ready yet," Roddy said. "It's going to take a while to implement. See, it hasn't been debugged yet, and—''

"You're disappointing me, Roddy," Rachel said, in a tone of voice that began to make him nervous. "I was expecting you to bring me a functional implementation. Instead you bring me a sketch . . . a blueprint. How am I supposed to show this to Gridley and then convince him not to toss you in front of a grand jury right after lunch?"

Roddy blanched. "No! I mean, no, it's all right, if you want to run it right away, test it on somebody, sure, I understand, but after all these changes, it may not—'' He stopped, seeing the look in Rachel's eyes. "Well, yeah, I guess it should run. It's run okay so far. But you're going to need the other half of the syndrome. The bug. The only one I've done was the one that worked on Alain, I hadn't . . . gotten . . .''

He trailed off suddenly.

"Gotten what?" Rachel said sharply.

"Uh," Roddy said, and then he smiled very slightly. "Well, there were a couple of other 'infections' working in prototype. They didn't have any microorganisms involved in them, just sickness produced by mirroring: chemical imbalances that mimicked infections, the way Alain's did. Toxins without the bugs.''

Rachel held quite still for a moment. "You mean you were getting Alain's body to synthesize toxins like those that would have come from bacteria . . . but *without* actually having the bacteria themselves present?''

"Yeah. It's not as effective. They put you on kidney dialysis and filter them out. It's not usually something that would kill you unless the programmer, unless I set the dosage of toxin unusually high. . . .''

"How interesting," Rachel said. "All right. Do it both ways. Give me what data I'll need to have the necessary microorganism produced. It shouldn't take too long. Net Force has good genetics and bio people. When we test it, if it all works out the way you say, you'll be fine. We'll quickly come to an agreement with Gridley and the law enforcement people." Rachel looked up at the structure again. "Meanwhile, you run a demonstration of the toxin-based routine for me as soon as you can. Do you need time to get your target in here to get the 'mirroring' part of the program going and set the marker chemicals up inside them?''

"Oh, no," Roddy said, and smiled. "No problem there. It's all handled. They've already been. . . .''

Somewhat later, Rachel Halloran was back in her house on the shore, with the windows closed against an early-evening shower. Rain pattered half-heard against the screens as she sat in the chair by the computer in the living room and lined up her implant with it. After that wrenching adjustment to the virtual world, she saw another room, a richly dark one paneled in wood, with a big dark polished wooden desk at one end; a lamp with a green glass shade stood on the desk, casting light on various data solids and some paperwork on the desk. Behind that desk sat a young slender man whose face was not quite visible in the shadows. Through the windows behind him, night showed, with a few city lights glinting far below.

"Mikhail, it's almost more than we could have hoped for," Rachel was saying. "This tool could be used for all kinds of things. Timed assassination. Traceless elimination of large groups of people—"

"I know a few organizations that would be in favor of *that*," Mikhail said softly. "Identify the right gene in the target population, speak to the gene in the bug . . . and *bang*."

Rachel nodded. " 'The bullet that turns corners.' The weapon every covert has dreamed of since Ashurbanipal killed his thousands and hundreds of thousands. Mik, a lot of people will get very rich off this."

"So they will," Mikhail said, in a tone of voice that suggested to Rachel that he was already considering methods to make sure that the number of people getting rich was as limited as possible. "Any more little surprises coming from your source, do you think?"

"Hard to say. Apparently he did the groundwork for this in a couple of months, secondary to another project. The kid's a tremendous talent. None too stable, though."

"Oh? How so?"

Rachel shrugged at the prospect of one more damaged-childhood story. "Father died in an accident, mother's marginally employed and a harridan, unsupportive . . . the relationship's toxic at best. The kid's socially unsophisticated—though also a fast learner, and very flexible when he feels he's challenged by a peer. But easily upset too . . . especially when everything starts to seem like it's going out from under him. Where exactly *is* our guy at the comms company rerouting the kid's messages?''

''An 'answering service' with live screening. His mother's still getting her normal calls all right, not that she has many . . . not a lot of friends, apparently. We'll kill the service after your boy delivers the goods.''

''Fine. But a controller who could figure out how to run him properly would have an interesting asset for the future.''

That shadowy face could just be seen to smile. ''Rachel, you don't usually indulge yourself in this kind of sentimentality. If this kid has what you think he has . . . he becomes dispensable as soon as we have the working technology. The *first* thing we would need to do is cover our tracks.''

''Mmm, you're right, of course.'' She sighed. It would have been useful to her personally to be the controller running Roddy. Just the brief brushes they'd had so far told her that she had a good handle on him. But the stakes were unusually high on this job, as the payoff would be.

''So,'' Mikhail said. ''How soon can we get a prototype running?''

''As soon as you can get our local talent to tailor the right bug. Roddy suggests one of the intestinals.''

''*Coli* might be a good candidate,'' Mikhail said thoughtfully. ''Enough hypertoxic variants are turning up spontaneously that one more won't attract too much attention. Certainly no one will bother speculating that it might have been engineered. And if what you're telling me is right, we wouldn't want or need to use any one organism more than once.'' He thought about it, then said, ''Have you got a sample of little Roddy's DNA?''

Rachel smiled. ''My assistant took a swab off his teacup the other afternoon,'' she said. ''And he considerately shed a few hairs on the chair . . . along with various skin cells and so forth.''

''He really is a trusting boy, isn't he?''

''Aren't most of them at his age? Just as well, or some of

them might have tried to go to the real Net Force to check our bona fides, and we would have had to, shall we say, interfere. Fortunately it hasn't happened yet. Their little egos don't seem to want to cope with the idea that the real Net Force wouldn't be interested in them.''

''You may be right. All the same, if I'd just invented this particular technology, ego or no ego, *I* certainly wouldn't take any meetings in person.''

''My guess is that our young Roddy didn't quite think it through. I think this may be a routine problem for him. . . .''

''Very good. Then since he was kind enough to describe the mechanism to you, we shouldn't have too much trouble. I'll have our people get to work on the infectious agent, and provide you with a sample. If I understand the way this works, they'll need to do some engineering and then run the altered bacterium through a few generations to make sure it 'breeds true.' ''

Rachel had been doing some research. ''The engineering is an afternoon's work nowadays. As for the growing-out period. . . . If they use *coli*, it takes about twenty minutes a generation—that means about thirty-six hours from start to finish.''

''Fine. Have him set up his demonstration . . . and make yourself a lunch date with the young genius.''

''I'll take him somewhere nice,'' Rachel said.

''You may as well. It's on the expense account . . . and anyway, he won't be having that many more lunches afterwards.''

8

Several days after her talk with James Winters, Maj was in her "villa," cleaning the place up. Not that it needed more than a thought to have it *look* tidy, of course, but the cabinets and bookshelves and storage facilities she had scattered around were almost *all* looking like the Muffin's toy chests. She had been busy enough with real life for a good while that her virtual life had gotten a little messy. She'd spent the last few weeks checking the code in her sim that Roddy had tampered with, hoping to find evidence there in his little messages to her that would link him with the attack on Alain in some concrete, incontrovertible matter. She hadn't found it. Nor had she gotten the sim to run yet. She'd finally decided it was time to tackle a less daunting project for a while. So now she was cleaning up, sorting, chucking things out she didn't need anymore, and generally getting organized.

The sliding doors, which opened onto the outside, were wide open and unopaqued now, so that the view from the cliff where the villa was built spread out beneath her and away to the burning western horizon. Blue water, three shades of blue in the sunset, gray cliffs, and far away across the harbor the twilight-dimmed, whitewashed masonry cube shapes and rounded roofs of the local fishing village. That was all there was to be seen. Low in the sky, a crescent moon hung, with Venus up above it: a lunar smile and a celestial wink.

Maj was in the fourth cabinet down on the west wall, chucking icons away into the "trash" behind her at some speed. *I can't believe I've let this stuff pile up this long,* she thought as she came up with various expired virt-mail coupons, long past even her mother being able to do anything about them, and numerous electronic "magazines" out of which she had doubtless meant to "clip" something—not that she could now remember exactly what she'd wanted to clip. She threw them away behind her, missing the trash can: The icons caught fire in mid-throw and appeared to burn up.

A knock on the door. She half turned, her arms full of icons of all shapes and sizes. "Come on in—"

Mark Gridley came in, looking around him curiously. They'd spent a good bit of time together lately working, though unsuccessfully so far, on the problem James Winters had set for them. Maj was always surprised by how small he was, even though they all called him "the Squirt." He was a slender, short, lithe kid of thirteen, his dad's Thai ancestry showing in his dark hair and deep brown eyes. "Hi," he said, and wandered past Maj, looking through the sliding doors. "Where is this?"

"Chios," she said, "the west side."

"Cleaning house? For me? Shouldn't have bothered."

Maj grinned at that. "The icons were getting a little thick in here, that's all."

"I know the problem," he said, and came to look over her shoulder at the drawer Maj was working on. It was at least somewhat less full than it had been. "Hey, this is neatness heaven compared to my space."

Somehow she found herself wondering about that. "Well, I've had enough of this for one day anyhow," Maj said. "I can only stand so much structure at one time." She leaned on the drawer with one hip, and it slid shut as she chucked the last few icons at the trash can.

"Good," Mark said. "By the way, my dad asked me to tell your dad hi."

Maj blinked. "Do they know each other? News to me." It was news, and slightly bizarre. Normally her dad refused to admit connection with any organization except the university, and governmental or quasi-governmental organizations usually caused him to wrinkle up his face and become strangely un-communicative.

Mark shrugged. "Probably one of those cocktail-party things," he said. "Not my problem. But as for problems," he said, and reached into his pocket, coming up with one of the blue-glass "map" tabs from the Funhouse, "I'm ready when you are."

"Great," Maj said. "Do you want to go in anonymized?"

Mark thought about that for a moment, then shook his head. "Probably no point in it," he said. "If your buddy doesn't know by now that someone's looking into his playroom with an eye to figuring out how it ticks, he doesn't have the brains that God gave a pill bug. He has to have half the proprietary-software companies on the planet snooping around in there, every one of them anonymized, and he's probably using up a lot of precious processing time following them around. Probably someone *un*anonymized will attract less attention. Besides, I have something they don't have."

"Oh?" Maj said, heading over for the doorway which, when she opened it, would let them into the main entrance hall of the Funhouse. "What's that?"

"His service provider's passwords to let me into his code area," Mark said. "By the terms of his contract, he can't stop them or their designated representatives from looking around in there." He smiled a small smile, which suddenly reminded Maj of the Muffin's apparent pleasure at the idea of the rotten things getting out of the fridge and coming after her. "And funny, but that's just what we are today. Rank hath its privileges. . . ."

Maj opened the door. They looked into the "entry area" of the Funhouse, the space into which Maj had gone with the Group of Seven the other night. Maj hesitated. "What if he's in there?" she said softly.

"He's not," Mark said. He held up the tablet again. "The provider sensitized this for me. If he shows up in the space, it'll yell. But my sources say he's off at a business meeting somewhere this morning."

"Sources," Maj said as they walked through the door and she shut it behind her. It vanished. "Must be nice having a whole network of enforcement people to play with."

They walked along through the entry hall, nodding to the various aliens they encountered. "It has its moments, yeah," Mark said, and grinned. "Can't wait to be old enough to play with them for real."

Maj glanced at him and nodded. On this at least they were in complete agreement. She only wished that her chances of "playing with" the rest of Net Force were as good as Mark's were.

They walked for what seemed about a mile and a half until they found a gallery that was deserted by both "aliens" and real people in virtual guises. "This'll do," Mark said, walking over to one of the shining stone walls and putting his hand up to it. In that hand was the blue glass tab.

His hand went through the wall. "Come on," he said to Maj, holding out his hand to her.

She took his hand. Mark stepped into the wall, and vanished. Maj took a breath and stepped through the wall after him.

At first nothing was visible but empty darkness . . . then, slowly, light began to grow around them.

"My gosh," Maj said, as the vista before her began to be visible. It was all she could think of to say.

When she had been very young, her father had brought out a toy he said he had played with when he was tiny. It was a can of "pick-up-sticks," delicate thin plastic sticks of many colors, all pointed at both ends. You shook the can and dumped the sticks out on the floor, and then started carefully removing them from the structure one at a time. The object of the game was to not be the one who pulled out the stick that made the structure collapse.

Now she found herself staring at what appeared to be a massive cubical structure maybe a half mile on a side, made of pick-up-sticks in a hundred colors and a thousand different lengths, all stuck with great care through and among one another. It was the graphic representation of Roddy's basic structural program for the Funhouse . . . and it made no sense to Maj at all. Worse, it suggested that touching or messing with anything would bring the whole structure down around them . . . and that would destroy what they were looking for, the code that had given Alain Thurston meningitis.

"I hope you can make something of this," she said, "be
cause it's Greek to me."

"You can't speak Greek?" Mark said, walking slowly
down the side of the great cube that was closest to them
"With that island and all?"

Maj shook her head ruefully. "Enough to ask where th
bathroom is, and whether there are sharks today."

He threw her a glance. "Sharks? Cool." He walked or
looking up at the cube. "Well, you work with authoring tool
that manipulate this stuff, so you wouldn't see it often. It'
virtual machine language, all right, but not one of the eas
ones. A language called Caldera."

"Do you know it?"

"Oh, yeah," Mark said, walking on a little faster, so tha
Maj had to hurry slightly to catch up with him. "Net Forc
uses it in some of their sims. It's good for packing a lot o
data into a tight space, which I'd guess is why your Rodd
got interested in it. Each of these"—he reached out towar
the end of one "stick," and it briefly fluoresced, silhouettin
a long series of darker colored dots down its length—"is
series of linked instructions, like several lines of code in ol
Basic. But each line is influenced more or less directly by th
other 'sticks' in direct contact with it. Move a stick and th
program runs differently." He stopped for a moment, with hi
hands on his hips, leaning back to look right up toward th
top of the construct.

"These constructs are nasty to debug," Mark said. "Or t
tamper with. Any stick, when moved, remembers the circum
stances under which it was moved."

"So if you move one—he'll know that you did it."

"He'll know somebody did it," Mark said. "But he won'
know who. As far as I can tell, he doesn't have any securit
enabled inside this space. He probably doesn't expect anyon
to be able to get in. The password protection from the outsid
is massive. And if he's got any logging facilities running,
can disable them."

Maj had to laugh softly at that. "No security, huh."

Mark's grin went ironic. "Yeah," he said. "I heard abou
what happened to your sim. Maybe we can return the favor.'

"Not by crashing his—"

"No," Mark said. "Something better, possibly . . ."

Mark trailed off for a moment, looking up at the vast program structure. "But we shouldn't have any trouble doing anything we find necessary, security or no security. Even if he's found a way to build in safeguards against unauthorized change into the program itself, they won't make much difference. While he's not here, even the best safeguards can only ape what Roddy would do if he anticipated a specific action. I'm betting I can find out what's going on in here without doing it in a way he'll have anticipated. If he has anticipated something I do, then we cut and run." He grinned, a slightly feral look.

"If it's any use by then," Maj said. "He's a slicker customer than you might think."

"Well, we'll see," Mark said. They started walking again, and went on for some time in silence while he studied the program structure. "I wish I had a better idea of what we were looking for specifically here," Mark said. "I mean, structurally speaking. This is real needle-in-a-haystack stuff."

" 'Looking for' in what way?"

"Well, in terms of the exact mechanism that Roddy used to affect your friend Alain. Virtual routines shouldn't be able to directly affect someone's physical status. I'm not sure what routines would look like that could affect it, but probably not very normal." He sighed and kept walking.

"Alain apparently went to see him in here one time," Maj said, "and watched him work."

"Knowing Roddy—not that I do," said Mark, "but from your description, I don't think he'd have let Alain see anything that he would have been able to understand."

"I don't know. . . ." Maj thought back to the night of the Funhouse opening. "You know, there was something funny Alain said when he got sick, it stuck in my mind . . . it didn't sound too much like raving. He started talking about threads—no, webs—"

"Did he," Mark said rather suddenly. "Now that's a thought. All this stuff looks so *linear*, doesn't it?"

"Yeah."

"Let's see. Control structure routine," Mark said.

"Here," said a voice in the air. Maj jumped. It was Roddy's voice.

"Fade down the master structure. Fade up all anomalous or nonlinear routines."

The huge structure of sticks faded away to grayness. Buried inside it, tangled, were hundreds of weblike, writhing threads, which now began to glow in many colors.

"Innnnnteresting," Mark said, and started walking again toward the half-mile-distant corner of the cube where many of those strings and threads seemed to knot together.

Maj kept up with him as best as she could. When they reached the corner, Mark paused and passed a hand over one of the strings that lay nearest the cube's surface, buried some three feet within. It glowed in response, showing itself dotted as the sticks were with splotches of darker color in intricate patterns down its length.

"Look at all this," Mark said. "It's code again. See the way it repeats? Always the same six shapes, different colors. What has a code like that?" He was starting to grin again.

It took her a moment. "DNA!" Maj said.

"Somebody's," Mark said. "Or something's. Wanna bet some of this is Alain's?"

She shook her head. "I wouldn't take your money," she said. It was all too easy to get DNA samples from a person. A strand of their hair let fall casually would be more than enough.

"Maybe not his directly," Mark said then. "But a copy of it, a match of part of it. And maybe not this strand—but one of these."

"And whose are all these others?" Maj said, somewhat unnerved, looking up at what seemed hundreds of other strands all twined together.

"You got me," Mark said. "But I bet that something more's going on here than just some practical joke. Look at this." He pointed at the way a given structure of sticks surrounded one of the strands near its end. "These aren't just assembly calls to the master sim program, like most of the other sticks here. They're calls to assemble certain specific *chemicals*. You see stuff like this in factories, or in microcontruction.'' He shook his head. ''Specific chemicals. But what hemicals, where?''

''If there's DNA involved? In something alive. Somebody's ody?'' Maj said.

Mark paused for a long moment, then nodded. ''Could be.''

She breathed out in bemusement. ''But instructions like that lon't make sense. They shouldn't work. They shouldn't be ible to cross the mind-body barrier.''

''No. But it looks like he *is* making them cross. Look here.'' Mark pointed at a spot where the meandering thread became entangled around several sets of ''sticks.'' ''That particular structure keeps happening. It's a neurotransmitter. He's instructing the body to take it apart and put it together a different way—and then that instruction makes something else happen, somewhere else in the body. Maybe something that eventually seems completely unconnected. You ever see those old cartoons? A candle burns through a string with a weight attached, and the weight falls on a teeter-totter, and that throws a ball in the air, which hits a chicken in the head and makes it lay an egg, which falls in a frying pan—''

''Heath Robinson,'' Maj said.

''No. I mean, yes, but I was thinking of Rube Goldberg. He did that kind of thing too. This might be how Roddy's doing it. He's not trying to go directly through the barrier. He's using all these end-runs and subroutines to trick the barrier itself into *believing it's not there.*''

Maj tried to get her head around that one. ''That is *so strange.* I'm not sure I believe it. . . .''

''I'm not sure *I* believe it either,'' Mark said, ''and that's what scares me about it. Even when I see it right in *front* of me, I'm not sure. Roddy's tricking the body into thinking it's part of the computer, part of the virtual routine. He's using neurotransmitters to do it . . . mimicking a phenomenon like 'entanglement' in photophysics, where you change the qualities of a photon and a neighboring photon changes too as a result . . . even though they're not touching. He's using something like that to execute changes at the molecular level . . . I think.''

''You *think*?''

Mark looked disappointed at having to make the admission,

but he said, "I'm no medical specialist. I'm not dead sure wha
I'm looking at here. Some of the chemicals Roddy's working
with molecular weights up in the hundreds o
thousands. . . ." He shook his head. "But whatever this is al
about, it's got to involve more than just Alain. There's no way
one joke played on him would need all *this* stuff." He waved
at the massive tangle of threads wound in among the sticks o
more conventional code. "Something much bigger is going on
here, more serious. Maybe something more dangerous."

Maj shivered.

"Come on," Mark said, "let's get out of here. This is giv
ing me the creeps."

Maj was glad not to have said it herself, possibly making
herself look like she didn't have what it took. They began
retracing their steps to where they'd come in. "So what are
we going to do now?" she said. "Winters is going to want a
report."

"He's going to have to wait for it," Mark said. "We don'
have all the data yet."

"Are we going to have to come back here?" Maj said. She
didn't relish the prospect. Normally she would have said there
was no aspect of Net life too weird for her to handle . . . bu
this place was giving her shivers, for reasons she didn't un
derstand.

"At least once," Mark said. "I want to bring some help
with us. You know Charlie Davis? He's another Explorer. He
lives up in D.C., goes to Bradford Academy. A serious med
ical type. He might be able to help us out here."

"Sounds like a good idea," Maj said. She was beginning
to have serious thoughts about this whole situation. If Roddy
could do this kind of thing to Alain without Alain even being
aware of what was happening to him—then there was no tell
ing who *else* he might do such things to. Who else was he
angry at? Would he stop at hurting just that person—or migh
he also be interested in hurting the people around them?

Maj's parents? Maj's brother? Her little sister?

"Let's find him and get him in here," she said. "Righ
away."

They passed back through the soft wall, and out into the
hallway again. She threw the door to her villa open, and wen

through it in a hurry, noting the odd way Mark was looking at her, and not caring.

The door closed behind them. Mark let out a long breath. "Okay," he said. "Want me to go get Charlie and bring him here?"

"No, I'll come with you."

"Fine."

They headed for the door together. "But one thing," Maj said as they went. "What was 'something better' supposed to be?"

Mark grinned, a totally evil look. "You being in the heart of his sim, with password access that would have allowed you to do anything you liked to it, including completely crashing it . . . and you *didn't* crash it. Let him try to figure *that* one out."

Maj shrugged. "He'll think I'm a wimp, is all."

"Oh, no. Not anymore. He's going to know you were here . . . and it's going to drive him crazy." Mark's grin got more evil, if possible. "As far as Roddy's concerned . . . you've become *dangerous*."

As they went out her "front door," heading for Mark's own virtual space, Maj found herself wondering whether that was entirely a good thing. . . .

9

When Maj and Mark finally found Charlie, he was sitting in his virtual workspace, doing his homework. Normally this would not have aroused much comment from anyone, but his workspace turned out to be the old Royal College of Medicine central lecture hall—all shining old-wood paneling and antique benches arranged in a circular amphitheater configuration, under a noble skylighted Palladian dome. And in the center of it all, Charlie was sitting there with his books and paperwork and printouts and logic solids spread out on the dissection table in the middle. He looked up as they came in, and said, "Mark?"

"In the flesh, if you'll excuse the word."

"Thought you said you weren't coming back in here anymore," Charlie said, looking up at him with a slightly wicked expression.

"Yeah, well, business," Mark said.

Maj looked around at the lovely space, admiring it. "Why wouldn't you want to come in here?"

"He showed me what they used to *do* in here Tuesdays and Thursdays," Mark said, resolutely looking away from the dissecting table. "Shouldn't happen to a dog."

"But it did," Charlie said, "repeatedly." He pushed the books to one side, then indicated a couple of nearby chairs: Chippendales, Maj thought, to judge by the backs. Her mother would have given all kinds of eyeteeth, her own or other people's, for the originals of these. "So tell me what's up," Charlie said.

They told him. When they were done, Charlie was looking at the table with a curious unfocused look that Maj thought was probably the result of trying to put a lot of peculiarly assorted information together in a hurry.

"Okay," he said. "You're suggesting that Roddy has somehow found a way to transmit infectious agents through the Net."

"Maybe," Maj said.

"Or to mimic the effects of infection—again via the Net."

"Something like that," Maj said.

Mark snickered. "Being cautious today . . ."

"Well, I'd better," Maj said.

"No, she's right," Charlie said. "Without more data, it's going to be hard to tell. We'd better go see the client."

"The client?"

"Alain. Who else? Though maybe," Charlie added after a moment, "not the only one. Maj, can you get through to him?"

"Whether anybody can get through to Alain is a good question," Maj said, "though if you mean 'can we reach him,' I have his code. We can see if he's in his space."

"Okay. Callout," Charlie said. "Maj, give it the code."

Maj rattled off the string of letters and numbers that would let her into her virtual communications address book, and then said, "Alain Thurston."

Immediately, from the air around them came a voice saying, "No visitors now, sorry." It was Alain's voice, his automated answering system.

"Alain, it's Madeline Green," Maj said. "I've got a couple of friends with me—we think we might be able to help with the Roddy problem."

"No visitors now, sorry," Alain's system said.

Charlie and Mark looked at each other. "Come on, Alain," Maj said. "I know you probably feel pretty awful, but it's not going to get any better until someone does something. My friends and I are Net Force Explorers, and we think we may be able to work out what to do."

There was a pause. At least no voice immediately said, "No visitors now, sorry."

Then the air around them shimmered, and the surroundings changed from the Royal College surgical hall to a beach. White sand, blue water, and bluer sky, a fringe of palm trees behind them, and sitting off to one side, with a umbrella made of palm fronds overhead, in one of those big wicker chairs with a wicker table to one side, sat Alain. He looked at them somewhat sourly as Maj and Mark and Charlie approached.

"Thanks for seeing us," Maj said.

Mark looked around with interest. "Nice beach," he said.

"Yeah," Alain said, with no interest in the compliment whatever. "The Maldives. Life's a beach, isn't that what they used to say? Mine was. Until recently. I keep this bit, as a reminder."

He looked at Maj even more sourly. "What I don't understand," he said, "is why you give a damn, after what I did to *you.*"

"Huh?"

"I got Roddy started on your sim. Little knowing, of course, what would happen. Or what he would do next. Why should you care if *my* life goes to pieces as a result?"

Alain's attempt, however slight, to make Maj feel sorry for him, annoyed her. "Look," she said, "let's just chalk it up to stupid blind altruism, if you like. Or a weird sense of revenge. Or whatever makes you more comfortable, since I'm not going to waste my time arguing situational ethics with *you*. This is Mark Gridley and Charlie Evans. We're all Net Force Explorers."

"Yeah," Alain said, not looking nearly as impressed as Maj thought he should have. "Yeah, should have known Net Force'd be after *me* next."

Maj blinked at that, but said nothing.

"So what have you got?" Alain said.

"Some ideas," Charlie said, "but first I need to know about any contacts you've had with Roddy L'Officier. Physical ones."

"None," Alain said.

"None at all?" Maj said. "You weren't at the Group of Seven pizza dinner he came to?"

"No, my folks took me to some dumb opera that night," Alain said with a put-upon look.

"So you've never physically met him at all," Mark said.

"Nope."

"How many virtual contacts?" Charlie said.

"Since I've met him? Maybe a few dozen."

"Any physical contact during those?"

"No," Alain said, looking at Charlie a little strangely. "Look, are you saying that you think I'm a—"

"I mean, have you played virtual sports with him, or something like that? Anything that would mean you bumped into each other?"

"Sports?" Alain laughed out loud. "Roddy isn't exactly the sports type. Neither am I."

"Okay." Charlie thought for a moment, then said, "Have you been in his workspace?"

"Sure."

"Lately?"

"Yeah, once, about a week and a half ago."

"Did he do or say anything unusual?"

"Hey," Alain said with a grimace. "This is Roddy we're talking about here. He's always a little unusual."

"And he didn't touch you then either. Shake your hand or anything."

"You don't get meningitis from shaking people's hands," Alain said, annnoyed. "Or from doorknobs either, now I come to think about it."

Mark turned away a little, ostensibly to admire a marlin leaping out of the water offshore, but Maj could see what Alain couldn't—his irritated expression. Charlie, though, was imperturbable. "And you didn't 'eat' or 'drink' anything while you were there."

"Not that he would have offered. It's not the kind of thing Roddy would normally think of—or, with his sense of humor, if he did think of it, you'd wish he hadn't."

"And you didn't touch anything else."

"For frack's sake, how can you avoid touching *something* in a virtual scenario?" Alain said. "That's the whole point—"

"With your bare skin," Charlie said, "or your hands."

"No, I wouldn't have—" Alain stopped. Maj glanced from

him to Charlie, and saw Charlie's eyes widen suddenly, just a little.

"Yeah," Alain said then, almost sounding a little surprised, as if this detail had gone entirely out of his mind. "He was weaving light into long strands . . . there was a big pile of it by his chair—he has this kind of 'throne' that he sits in. He gave me some of that stuff to hold . . . a piece of what he was working with. It looked like rope . . . but all twisted together."

"How many twists?"

"Two," Alain said. "And there were pieces between the twists, like the rungs of a ladder. It looked like—"

"DNA," they all said together, and Mark looked at Maj rather wide-eyed.

"He *can't*," Maj said, almost rebelliously. "Not with real DNA anyway. They're hardly anywhere near finished with the Human Genome Project, at least not discovering what each gene does, for creep's sake, and anyway, even if it was all finished and every gene was classified by site and function, you can't just pull DNA apart and stick it back together like Tinkertoys!"

"Well, you can," Mark said. "Using microsurgery. But not virtually." He stopped, and added, "Not *yet*."

"Bets?" Maj said.

Mark looked at her with an expression she had seen once or twice now on James Winters: instant acceptance of a very unpleasant reality.

"He gave you some to hold," Charlie said to Alain slowly. "That's interesting. And that was all?" he said.

"Yeah," Alain answered back. "I chucked it back to him. That was it."

"Okay," Charlie said. "I think that's how he made you sick. All we have to do is find some evidence of exactly what that fragment was to figure out why it worked." He glanced at the others. "We should go check out that space you told me about, Mark—then I'll have a better idea."

"Right."

"Okay. Alain, if we need to see you later—"

"I'll be here," Alain said, plainly trying to sound both mildly interested and completely uncaring at the same time. "I'm not going anywhere now. Maybe never."

They nodded.

"Oh, and tell Rachel I said thanks," Alain added.

"Rachel?"

"Halloran. She's at Net Force."

"Sure."

"Recall," Charlie said very quietly.

They were back in his space again.

Mark let out a breath. "Mads, I hate to say it, but at the moment this guy seems to me like one of the world's great candidates to be made sick by remote control. What a waste of time!"

"He's scared and upset," Maj said, "and worse, he's done something really stupid, and he thinks that everybody knows. And I'll grant you, he has the manners of someone with a hedgehog up their . . . Let's leave it at that for the moment. What are you thinking?"

"Nothing I can share until I've seen Roddy's workspace," Charlie said. "Meanwhile, who's Rachel Halloran?"

"Must be somebody with Net Force," Maj said. "Maybe somebody working with James Winters?"

Mark blinked, then shook his head. "Not a name I recognize." He shrugged. "Then again, there are five thousand people in the organization, and more all the time . . . she's probably new. Never mind, we'll take care of it later."

"Okay." Mark activated the passwords that would take them into Roddy's space. The air went dark around them, then brightened again to the clear glow of the "entry hall." Mark studied his blue glass chip closely.

"He's not here?"

"He was here a while ago, according to this. Gone now," Mark said.

"Good, let's check this construct out."

A few minutes later they were in the huge, dark space that Maj was coming to think of as the Temple to the God of Pick-Up-Sticks. Charlie just stood quietly at first, gazing up at the program structure.

"I take it," he said, "that there was something you saw in here that made you think I should be involved."

"Yeah," Mark said. "There's a lot of neural chemistry going on in here. Come check this out."

They walked on down past the same side of the towering cube that Maj and Mark had walked past before. Mark was studying the little blue chip. Maj looked over his shoulder at it curiously. While Mark held it and looked down at it, Maj could see, as if in the air "below" it, lines and lines of data scrolling by.

"Access logs," Mark said as they walked. "See, there we are—and here we are again."

"But there's another access 'between' our two," Maj said.

Mark nodded. " 'Proprietor and guest,' " he read.

"Guest?" Maj said. "Now who else would Roddy let in here? Not Alain, I'll bet."

Mark shook his head. "Interesting," he said, and paused for a moment. "Here, Charlie. Program."

"Working," said Roddy's voice.

"Highlight all anomalous or nonlinear constructs."

Most of the contents of the cube faded down to near-invisibility again. Charlie looked at the swirls and curves of data.

"I know Caldera a little," he said dubiously, "but not as well as you do. Can you give me this data in some other configuration?"

"Not the programming," Mark said. "But the straightforward references to the chemicals, yeah. Stickball?"

"Yeah, that's fine."

The rest of the cube faded away almost completely now, leaving them looking at a tangle of molecular models, atom-balls joined together by virtual dowels representing chemical bonds. Maj looked at the huge tangle of it. The appearance of all these structures was now much more daunting to her than it had been before. But Charlie was walking down the side of the cube, pausing every now and then, taking it all in, and he didn't seem daunted at all.

"You're right about the neural stuff," he said, pausing by one huge complex of molecules. "The neurotransmitters are having a regular party here. Half the paracrine family . . . serotonin, the serotinin metabolites, a ton of lipophilics . . . monoamines especially. Look at them all. Something's going on with the sympathetic nerves here. Yeah, neuropeptide Y . . ."

Mark, sauntering along behind him, made a face. "Want to break for a moment and let us have that in English?"

"Hard to talk specialist subjects without specialist vocabulary," Charlie said mildly. "But this much even you should be able to understand, oh biologically challenged one. Someone's messing with the outer limits of neurochemistry here. The parts of it that have to do with unconscious and autonomic functions, stuff like breathing and digestion . . ."

"And immune response?" Maj said.

Charlie glanced at her, then nodded. "At one remove. But the nerves are really where the action is, and the effect they have on glandular action, or vice versa."

He stopped suddenly. "This picture's too small," Charlie said. "Let's try something else. Mark, all this chemistry leads up into bigger structures."

"Yup."

"Okay. These are the building blocks. Let's see what the cranes look like—get a glimpse of what this guy's building."

He rattled off a string of instructions that didn't make much sense to Maj, but which Mark nodded at. The configuration of the contents of the cube changed again. This time the network that twisted through it looked more delicate, and more involved.

Charlie walked around the corner of the cube and down the far side, studying it, then said to Mark, "I think I need to have this whole configuration rotate ninety degrees right—what would be the command for that?"

"Strangely enough, ninety right in x," Mark said. The whole huge construction shimmered, vanished, then appeared again, now "lying" on the face they had just walked along before turning the corner. "Uh-huh," Charlie said, and started walking once again in the same direction he had been going before.

"Uh-huh," he said again after about a minute, as they followed him, and he was starting to sound angry. "Look at it. See those? They're synapses. Look at all of them. *It's a nervous system.* No, it's worse. It's a *template* of a nervous system. The structure is the same, but the only thing that has to change is the DNA involved in the nerve cells. And you can change that. It's exactly the same kind of search-and-replace function that computers are best at. Swap out one person's DNA and messenger RNA, swap in another's, all in one function . . . and then operate on them. Oh, my God . . .''

Charlie walked on down the structure, holding out his hands to various of the delicate weblike lines of light where they swerved near the surface. They lighted as his hand moved near them. "See that. It's not even a *whole* nervous system—just the best bits of the central. Not the whole brain. Just the stuff you really need for basic maintenance and protein synthesis. The pineal and the pituitary glands, the corpus callosum, the cerebellum. The brain stem, and then the spine and the ganglia serving the spinal nerves. But nothing else. Why just *this*?''

He walked further. "Form follows function," Charlie said, thinking out loud. "It's not about cerebration. It's a chemistry set. It's about glandular secretion—messenger chemicals, messenger modulation—"

"There's more neurotransmitter chemistry stuff over here," Mark said.

Charlie went to join him, and looked at the structures Mark had highlighted. "Acetylcholine," he said, "yeah, ADP, TDP, GABA: the oligomers, the radioligands and the protein kinases . . . oh, *jeez*.''

"But why build a replica of someone's central nervous system?" Mark said. "Or just of pieces of it? To make it think it's a real nervous system?"

Charlie stood and stared. "Or to make a real nervous system think it's *this* one."

They all stood briefly mute, looking at each other.

"And then what?" Charlie said.

"Manufacture chemicals inside them," Maj said. "Custom chemicals. You could do all kinds of things . . . like make the person sick.''

"Toxins," Mark said. "Bacteria give those off when they get inside you.''

"You could build them from fragments of available proteins, if you were really clever," Charlie said. "And this guy's really clever. It would even look like an infection . . . one that didn't respond to the antibiotics. There are plenty of those around. Oh, creeps.''

He looked like someone who had been forced to eat some-thing disgusting.

"This is really awful," Charlie said. "This technology could be used for all kinds of things. There are *cancer* cures here!—if someone knew about them—"

It was getting a little too much for Maj. "You mean to tell me that the best brains in the world," she said, "people trying to do *good,* I mean, have been trying for years to work this stuff out, and failing—and *this* kid, looking to play a nasty practical joke, manages it where they *haven't*?"

"Yup."

"It's not fair!"

"Whoever said anything was fair?" Charlie said, but he looked annoyed and grim as he said it. "Never mind. It's all here. Now we have to figure out what to do about it . . . and all this stuff over here. This isn't cell structure, or a template for it. It's DNA." He walked further on down the side of the cube, nearly to one corner, where he paused again. "Look at that." They looked. It was plain that he was right, for the double-helix pattern stretched far off into the center of the cube, in many strands.

"DNA from who?" said Mark.

Charlie shook his head. "This piece, I'd say more like 'what.' I think it's bacterial."

"A virus, maybe?" Mark said. "A genuine one?"

Charlie thought about that for a moment, then shook his head. "No, this looks more complex than that. But also, if I were in his position, I wouldn't bother. Viruses are stupid. Oh, stop that, I know it looks obvious. What I mean is, viruses aren't very adaptable unless you specifically *build* them that way . . . and most people aren't very good at that.

"Viruses in the wild, now that's another story. They have hundreds and thousands of generations to adapt themselves within just a year. But tailored viruses tend to stay the way they are and *not* mutate . . . because that's the last thing the people building them want them to do while they're still in the lab. And you can't have it both ways. Either a virus is tame or wild, shortly after its inception. A tame one can easily go wild later in its life, after a few hundred thousand generations . . . but it still won't be as adaptable as one that's been wild forever.

"Look at AIDS. *That* was a wild one originally, and every time they got hold of the little monster, it would mutate and leave them standing there cursing, while the virus itself ran off laughing and infected a few million more people."

"Okay," Mark said, "so what would you use?"

"Bacteria," Charlie said. "They're lots 'smarter.' They're easy to mutate fast. They're really easy to tailor. Maybe too easy, if you ask me. You can do it in a petri plate in the fridge." He grinned. "I've done it myself. One of my chemistry instructors was involved in bio—"

"Biology?"

"Biological warfare," Charlie said gently. "He told us, 'Why screw around with viruses? It's really easy to make a bacterium more virulent. First you get it to . . .' " He stopped. "No, never mind."

"Chicken," Mark said.

"You betcha," said Charlie. "I know *I* can be trusted with the information, but can *you*?"

Mark rolled his eyes. "We'll never know now."

"Nope. But bacteria . . . there are hundreds of families of them that specialize in fast infection that doesn't kill the host at the same time. That's the problem with viruses. They're too simple, by and large, and a lot of them don't know how to do anything but kill their hosts. The ones that don't are just inept. Bacteria now, they're generally smarter. Mostly they keep you alive while they breed inside you . . . they've learned it's smarter not to kill the host that carries you around to new hosts elsewhere. From the looks of things, I'd say your friend is looking to hook this technology to a vector—something that'll let him use it as a 'time bomb.' More controllable that way." Again Charlie looked infinitely disgusted, his expression that of someone seeing a tool for great good used for loathsome purposes.

"Okay," Mark said. "It was meningitis Alain came down with anyway. That's bacterial, isn't it?"

"Yeah, usually. But . . ." Charlie rubbed his hands together slowly. "Okay, there are lots of meningococci. But they tend to be specialized, and they're a little fragile . . . sensitive to eat and drying. And more to the point, not everyone carries them. To avoid being noticed at all, I'd use something everyone carries."

"*E. coli,*" Maj said suddenly.

Charlie nodded. "Yeah," he said, "or one of the other families of intestinal flora that live in all our guts. But *coli*'s everywhere else too . . . as they started finding out a couple of decades ago, when the species got frisky and started turning up those hypertoxic strains. You can't disinfect the whole planet, or stand around staring at everyone's colon to see if something's mutating inside them."

He stood back from the construct for a moment and folded his arms, looking up. "Anyway, I'm pretty sure this is bacterial DNA," Charlie said. "It's only about an eighth of a mile long. But these . . ." He pointed at several other strands. "Much longer. These are human. Or I'd bet money they are anyway. They're a lot more complex, and why would Roddy waste time with animal DNA? Given his apparent interests." Charlie shrugged. "One of them's your friend Alain's, I think. The others . . ." He shook his head. "Anyway, as far as the bacterial end of things goes, I can find out what's going on in about five minutes. The *coli* genome has been mapped for a long time. It's one of the lab bacteria that people experiment on most. I can tie into my workspace and do a comparison, find out if this really is *coli* or one of its friends, and which strain. This other stuff . . ." Charlie was looking at the DNA strands again. "I don't know," he said.

Then Charlie suddenly opened his mouth and shut it again a couple of times, which made him look rather like a fish, though Maj didn't say so. Finally he said, "Madeline, something you said to Alain . . . *you've* met this guy Roddy, right? Physically, I mean."

"Huh? There was nothing physical about it."

"I don't mean *that*. I mean, you've met him non-virtually."

"Huh? Oh. Yeah, once. Not too long ago. The Group of Seven decided to have a get-together specifically because a lot of us had never met anywhere but virtually. So most of us got together over at Passionate Pete's Pizza and Pasta Emporium."

Mark clutched his head. "The place with all the antique Formica? My God. What taste you have."

"Taste, yes, in my mouth at least," Maj said. "I don't care about the furniture. I would have gone to a hole in the ground and sat on a rock to see someone bring Fergal a pizza that was too big for him to finish. It was amazing. He moaned when he saw them bringing it. Worth any amount of tacky furnishings. But Charlie, why does it matter if he . . ."

She trailed off.

"Did he by any chance do anything to get some of your DNA?" Charlie said.

"Huh? No, he never touched me."

"Think about it. What *did* he do?"

Maj thought. "Nothing. There was a lot of joking around, and he was drawing things on the napkins, he's a good artist really, and he . . ."

She stopped. Now it was her turn to open her mouth and close it again.

"Napkins, huh," Charlie said. "Slick. Paper ones, of course."

"Yeah," Maj said. "He got everybody's." She began cursing herself. It was a fairly simple way to get a mouth swab off somebody. Your odds of success were high, if not a hundred percent.

"Come on, Mads," Charlie said mildly. "Hindsight's twenty-twenty. You couldn't have known."

"It's not that," she said. But it *was*. Her DNA would have elements in common with her mother's, her father's, her sister's and brother's. *He could get at any of them. Any of them. Because of* me.

"The slimeball. The little slimeball!" Maj shouted. "I swear to God, I'll pull him to pieces, chuck him in a pot with some tar, boil him down, and pave a runway with him!"

"Inventive," Charlie said. "Let me know how it turns out. If it works, you could sell the technique to the Highway Department and get rich around pothole time. And as for you," Charlie said, looking over at Mark, "he's done something a little different."

"Oh, come on," Mark said. "How would he get my DNA?"

"Did you come in here anonymized the other night?"

"No. Why bother?"

"Uh-huh. So the son of the director of Net Force walks into
ddy's little lair, and Roddy's system alerts him that some-
e potentially interesting has come in—and he starts paying
rsonal attention. He instructs his system to start mirroring
u. It builds as much of the mirror as it can." Charlie looked
ound him. "How long were you in here?"

"About three hours. No, more like four."

"There you are then. I bet his system just kept interrogating
ur virtual body until it had a nice mirror built up. Then the
o systems ran in 'identity' for a while until he could get a
apshot of your DNA from some easily accessible source.
lls in your cerebrospinal fluid, I bet. There's always a lot
fragmented DNA floating around in there . . . and plenty of
e complete stuff. The computer just delegated some proc-
sing space and kept hammering away at your 'mirror' and
e 'unreal' you until it got the information it needed. Then it
ored it away."

"Sonofa—"

"Yup," Charlie said, looking up at the structure with an
easy expression. "You can never tell when it might be use-
l to have something on somebody at Net Force—that's what
's thinking, I'll bet. Well, now he does. And he can do
mething to you like he did with Alain. He doesn't even need
get a concrete sample of your 'non-virtual' DNA. He can
oduce the effects without it."

Charlie looked around them. "So now we need to ask one
estion. Does he have something like that, the mirroring soft-
are, running *in here*?"

Mark and Maj looked at each other.

"Uh-huh," Charlie said. "If I were on the paranoid side, *I*
re would. Anybody was in here besides me, I'd want some-
ing to use against them later if they messed me over. So we
ant to see what 'recordings' of DNA or other physical data
ight have been made in here recently. And then," Charlie
ded, "it's just possible that we may want to make some
anges. Because I bet you serious money that whatever little
esent he wished on Alain is ticking inside *you* two right
w."

Maj gulped, and stared at Mark.

Mark nodded, looking, Maj thought, entirely too co
about it.

"It's probably mirroring me too right now," Charlie adde
"If you can find that function for me—it's probably too la
for you two—it might be smart if you trashed it before t
mirror's complete. One of us has to be sure that we can repe
in on this."

"But for the rest of us," Mark said, "assuming Roddy ge
in here before we have a chance to come in for a third sessic
better he should think that nothing has been tampered with

He looked at Maj, and said nothing.

She gulped again. "Charlie," she said, "what about peop
with similar DNA to mine? Relatives?"

Charlie looked thoughtful. "The 'toxin' form of attack ca
hurt them," he said. "Noncommunicable. The vector, if
gets it tailored right . . . No." He shook his head. "The mat
wouldn't be close enough. He'd have to mirror them too."

"Leave it then," Maj said, and swallowed one more tin
feeling nearly as spitless as she had in the Valkyrie as it we
down.

"Right. Meanwhile, there's one other possibility we shou
investigate," Charlie said. "Leaving other people's DN
aside . . . if you were working with genetic material, and y
needed some to experiment with—what's the first place y
would look?"

Maj looked at Charlie . . . and started to grin.

"Yes," she said.

"You betcha," Charlie said. "That information should
in here too. And if Roddy can use his DNA, why can't w
Let's look for it. Other useful information will probably
nearby. But first . . . Mark, if I illustrated a chemical for you
could you build it in here?"

Mark interlaced his fingers and flexed them till the knuckl
cracked. "Try me," he said.

Charlie nodded. "Shouldn't do that, Mark. It's bad for yo
joints."

"So's death," Mark said mildly.

"Oh, okay, we'll worry about your joints later. Whi
chemical modeling orthography do you read easiest?"

"Uh, classic stickball, same as you were using."

"You got it. Meanwhile, you're going to need to program
e a fairly large structure as well. It's going to have to tie
to this one. I don't want it to be obvious to Roddy when he
nally turns up."

Mark grinned. "No problem there," he said, and glanced
p at the massive construct. "You know how many millions
f lines of code this would represent if it were printed out?
o programmer knows a program of *this* size well enough to
e able to hold it all in his head at once, or tell right away if
omething's wrong with it. I'll build what I'm doing right in
ith his stuff, in deep—and I'll assign it all time-stamps that
orrespond to the times he's most recently been working. Even
he instructs the program to display everything new when he
omes in next, he's not going to be clear about what's his and
hat's mine. His programming will be as much 'all over the
lace' as mine is. Leave it to me."

"If you're going to start getting involved in complicated
uff," Maj said, "give me that token. I'll stand guard."

Mark handed it to her, sat down cross-legged on the floor,
nd started manipulating the construct. Charlie got busy with
is own construction, another peculiar-looking piece of stick-
nd-ball architecture, occasionally coming over to consult with
Mark or to instruct him in something that needed doing.

This went on for what seemed like years, though Maj was
atching the elapsed-time counter in the token, and knew they
ad barely been there for an hour. The problem was that there
as little else for her to do now but watch them work, and
atch the token constantly for any sign of Roddy appearing.
Maj concentrated on not feeling useless and not getting in the
thers' way. It occasionally became difficult.

At one point, unable to resist, she wandered over to where
Mark sat and looked over his shoulder at a Caldera program-
ing structure he was altering, one "stick" at a time. She was
bout to say, *It looks complicated,* and then stopped herself.
here was probably nothing dumber that she could have said,
nd it would have been purely for the sake of making con-
ersation and trying to hide how nervous she felt.

After a few seconds Mark stretched and looked up at her.

Maj looked at what he had been doing, the alteration he ha
been making, and said, "It blends right in."

"That's part of it," Mark said, rubbing his eyes for a mc
ment and looking up at the structure. "But there's more to
than just that. You have to match the other guy's style, th
way he programs. A programmer of any experience can te
his own style, or someone else's. You know, the way the guy
who used to send telegrams via Morse code could get to knov
another telegraph operator by his 'fist,' the rhythm and trans
mission habits that that guy alone would use."

"Can't believe it," Charlie said suddenly from off to on
side. "This is human DNA, all right."

"You checked?"

"Well, I checked the *coli* first. It's a familiar strain . . . wit
some nasty changes. No problem there. This big long piec
here, though"—he reached into an extrusion of Roddy's con
struct—"this one actually has a little tag on the end of it tha
says M GREEN." He smiled sardonically. "One for you too
Mark. And Alain."

"Oh, God," Maj said.

"Nope, it's good news," Charlie said. "Now I know wha
Roddy was doing with Alain. He got him to touch that mirrc
of his own DNA to see if he'd gotten it right. And that starte
Alain's clock running."

"Does that account for all the DNA in here?"

"Nope, there's a few more strands, besides Roddy's own,
Charlie said. "Still working on them. And this one look
a little odd. Not sure what it is, at first look." He squinte
into the construct. "Either of you know somebody calle
'Fuzzy'?" Then he blinked. "Oh, looks like it's a hamste
Never mind—now I know where to get started. How you do
ing, Mark?"

"Getting there."

Charlie went back to his work. Mark took a breath, an
turned his attention back to his work, starting to play pick-up
sticks in reverse again. "This all may look okay to you," h
said to Maj, "but I've got to match Roddy's style close
enough that he won't notice the difference if he gets in her
and takes a close look." He started carefully altering anoth
"stick" of programming.

"He might *not* look," Maj said.

"That's not a chance I can take. Besides . . . I'd do it anyway."

"Seems like a waste of time."

Mark paused. "Well, maybe not. You know about the melon in the National Cathedral?"

"What?" Maj said.

"It looks more like a pumpkin really," Mark said, altering the position of another stick. "There are a lot of melons and vines all over the ornamental sculpture in the cathedral because some bankers, a family called Mellon, gave them a lot of money. It was some designer's joke. Anyway, some guy is carving one of these pumpkins, or melons, or whatever, and he's doing the back of one. Taking a long time." Mark paused, inserted another "stick," looked at it, and then reached out and slightly altered its position several times. "Somebody down on the cathedral floor sees this and yells at him, 'Why are you wasting your time? No one's going to see.' And the sculptor stops and looks at the pumpkin for a moment, and then yells back, '*God* will see.'"

Maj smiled slightly. "And the moral is?"

"Oh, jeez, Maj, cut it out." Mark squirmed just a little. "I just like to do good work, is all. It's stupid to do any other kind. Especially," he added, looking over his shoulder at Roddy's construct, "if it can get you killed. Or somebody else . . ."

"Especially," Maj murmured, and turned her attention back to the token, standing guard.

It lay flashing red in her hand, beat, beat, beat, like a frightened heart. *How long had it been doing that?!* "Guys," she said, *"trouble!"*

10

"So," Mikhail's voice said down the encrypted videophone line—though the current signal was strictly audio. He was apparently busy with someone else, not to be using visual so late in the day. "How's it going?"

"Everything's running smoothly," Rachel said, glancing out toward the beach grass beyond the house. It was rustling in a rising offshore wind. "Our boy's shown me a test run of the nonorganism-based 'infection.' I actually felt sorry for the gerbil."

"It's not gerbils we need at the moment. The buyers are lining up."

"I know. Roddy'll have two sick subjects for me to check tomorrow. He had to wait for them to slip into his space again to activate the process. It won't take long. He had them Trojaned already, the little monster. As soon as they come out, symptoms will show. I'm having their homes watched. We'll have no trouble getting a video record, and the records from the hospitals afterwards." And she chuckled. "You know who one of them is?"

"Should I care?"

"Gridley's son."

"Really?" There was a thoughtful chuckle at that. "Well, this *is* going to be one of life's little pleasures. Be amusing if someone at the hospital made a mistake."

"I wouldn't recommend going that far. If there's anything

we don't want at this point, it's for the situation to go high-profile.''

"I suppose. Still, it's a pleasant thought. . . . Meanwhile, your package is ready."

She chuckled. "I love the spy talk. As if anyone can hear us."

"Old habits die hard maybe."

"Good. I've already scheduled our lunch . . . tomorrow noontime."

"Fine. As soon as we have hard data on our pigeons, you can activate his version of the vector . . . and we'll have one less thing to worry about. Speaking of which, the boss wants you to stop in Riga on your way out this time."

"Oh? Problems?"

"No, something about a performance bonus."

Rachel smiled to herself. "Always nice to be appreciated. I'll take care of it."

He broke the link. Rachel sat back in the chair in the little beach house, wondering idly why Mikhail hadn't taken the call visually. That, combined with Riga . . .

Hmmm.

She had been in this line of work long enough to become pretty cautious . . . and it had occurred to her more than once that anyone associated with this particular project might well become a casualty themselves if they didn't step very carefully. *Until the "bugs" are worked out of this technique,* she thought, *personal meetings are a no-no.* Of course, *after* the bugs were worked out, there would be no significant difference between personal and virtual meetings. . . .

But who was he seeing that he didn't want me to see? Rachel thought. *Interesting . . .*

She sighed. This business had never exactly been a safe one, but that was one of the reasons she had gotten into it in the first place. The money made it worthwhile, and the spice of excitement was never missing. *Well, things will be getting exciting enough in the world when this gets loose,* she thought. *I might as well start packing. I won't have time after lunch tomorrow. . . .*

Rachel got up and headed for the bedroom to dig the suitcases out of the closet, and to begin the process of shutting the beach house down . . . most likely for the last time.

The air in the workspace literally began to tremble. A clap of thunder echoed overhead—and suddenly Roddy was standing there in front of them, his face full of fury, simply trembling with rage. *"Who let you in here!"* he screamed.

Maj held up the token and tried not to look as upset as she felt. "Who do you think?" said Mark very calmly, not even looking up from his work. "Your service provider got wind that something naughty was going on in here."

"You're trespassing! You're altering my work!" Roddy stormed over toward Mark, both fists lifted. "You're forgetting who's master of this sim! I can do anything I *like* to you!"

There were shapes moving in the darkness, just at the edge of vision. Maj got a glimpse of one of them . . . and it was just too much.

"You already *have,*" Maj said furiously, putting herself between Mark and Roddy, and surprising herself considerably as she did it. "You're screwing around with my nervous system, just the same way you screwed around with my sim." She began advancing on him. "Got in there, made a few little changes, thought it would be fun, huh? What was I supposed to learn from *this,* huh, Roddy, what little lesson? In what way was *this* for my own good? *Huh?*"

He was backing away from her, away from Mark, looking most astonished. It was satisfying, but not nearly satisfying enough.

"And all of us in the Group trying to be so nice to you, so fair. What a fracking waste. Well, you took it just a little too far this time," Maj said, stalking him. The dark shapes in the background, Roddy's creatures, didn't look inclined to come much closer. They scuttled back and away from their master, back into the shadows. "*Now* we get serious, you and I. I am personally going to teach you something about real life. A little lesson *not* about simming. If I live through this, you'll wish that you and *your* precious sim—"

"Forget the sim, it's not important," Charlie said.

"What?" said both Roddy and Maj, in rather incongruous

unison. Roddy's voice was more of a squeak, Maj's more of a bellow.

Charlie frowned at them both. "Are you deaf *and* dumb, L'Officier? I said, *Forget the sim.* What you've got here is *much* more important. The sim is *nothing* beside the 'mirroring' technology that it contains. That's almost the funny part, if there's anything funny about this after discovering that Maj and Mark are getting sick with a nonbacterial meningitis already, and didn't even know it."

Roddy gulped, and looked at the two of them guiltily.

"Yeah, we know all about it," Mark said. "You think you're the only person who ever worked in Caldera? Please, spare me. Oh, and something else," he said. "There is no Rachel Halloran."

"What? You're crazy, she's—"

"Not in Net Force," Mark said. "Trust me. My father runs it. I checked the personnel records, which, as you might imagine, contains all our operatives' 'working names' as well as their real ones. No one of that description, no one of that name."

Roddy looked utterly floored. This was plainly not a possibility that had ever occurred to him. *"Then who is she?"*

"There are people out there," Mark said, "who pretend to be Net Force for their own reasons. Sometimes it's just ego. Sometimes it's worse. This is worse. This lady has been using you and your work to develop a germ-warfare weapon. Do I have to spell it out any more clearly? She's going to sell your technology to the highest bidder. And then, to make sure they have control of it, to make sure no one else knows the details—"

Roddy's eyes went wide.

"I'm dead," he said. "Oh, my God."

"Roddy," Charlie said, turning his attention back to the vast mirroring construct, "lose the drama. There are more important things to be discussing. What you've done here is an *amazing* thing. With a little work, what you've invented can be a cure for cancer. Better than guided imagery, even with the counselor working with you virtually—better than tinkering with individual genes, better than all kinds of things. Cheaper, faster. I mean, not every cancer *everywhere* . . . but this work, properly tailored and altered, could work for about half the cancers we know about at the moment . . . and the others, with this head start, would all go the same way eventually.''

Charlie shook his head in astonishment. ''All kinds of immune-system therapies and hormone tailoring and I don't know what else can be done using this 'mirroring' technique you've found. You're the best guide to the ins and outs of it. You've got to be saved for this work. You've done something really amazingly bright here.''

''Yeah,'' Mark said very sourly. ''Now all we have to do is keep you from getting really amazingly *dead* as well. While continually asking ourselves why we shouldn't just beat the virtual 'you' into a pulp.''

He stood up, and Maj, who had for a while stopped noticing how small Mark was, suddenly noticed that, while he was no taller, he abruptly looked a lot bigger somehow as he in his turn slowly began to advance on Roddy. It also suddenly occurred to her that the son of the director of Net Force would most likely have had more than enough training to be very effective at the ''pulping'' part of this transaction, virtual or otherwise.

Roddy started moving backwards again, towards Maj this time. ''We're getting sick right now, aren't we?'' Mark asked. ''Our bodies anyway, back home. The minute we come out, we're going to start feeling the symptoms. We're going to wind up in the hospital, I think, no matter what happens— even if we deactivate your little private plague right now. Which we might as well, now that we're having this little conversation and you know we've been here.''

''But if you deactivate it—'' Roddy began.

''Might be nicer if *you* did that,'' Maj remarked.

''If *I* deactivate it,'' Roddy said, throwing Maj a look as fear-filled as the one he'd given Mark, and taking yet another step backwards as Mark kept coming, ''you won't get sick— any *sicker* anyway. You won't *have* to go to the hospital—''

''I know *I'm* going to want a checkup after this,'' Maj said, standing there with her arms folded and watching with grim amusement. ''You bet I'm going.''

''Besides,'' Charlie said suddenly, looking up from his

work again, "I'd say *those* two"—and he nodded at Maj and Mark—"are test cases. Wouldn't make much sense to have a test and not have anybody watching . . . would it now?" The look he turned on Roddy was cheerful enough, but it had an edge to it. "I bet your little Rachel-friend out there is going to have people keeping an eye on Mark and Madeline. If they *don't* get sick, the bad guys will know something's gone wrong, and everybody'll go to ground. Except maybe Rachel . . . and if Maj and Mark don't get sick enough to prove that you've done your part of the deal, I wouldn't be in your size sixes for anything." He looked back down at his work. "Not that I would anyway, frankly, but this isn't the time to deal with that. So?"

"I'll shut it down, I'll shut it down," Roddy said hurriedly, still backpedaling as Mark came toward him.

"I'm going to watch every move you make," Mark said. "One bad word out of you and . . ." He grinned. "But I don't know why you would try something so stupid, especially when we're going to save your butt."

"When we do get sick," Maj said, breaking out into a slight sweat at the thought—she hated being sick with a passion— "they'll think everything's going according to plan . . . and they'll go on with whatever else they have in mind."

"Rachel will come in here right after that," Mark said. "No matter what . . . if they've tailored a bug, she's got to come in here to tell the program about it, and introduce the 'mirror' version of the vector. And when she does . . ."

He grinned knowingly at Roddy. Roddy stopped in his tracks and stared back, looking frightened.

"You mirrored *her* when she came in, didn't you?" Mark said.

Roddy opened his mouth, closed it again.

"I don't believe you didn't," said Mark. "*Anybody* who came into this space, you set the trigger to mirror automatically. Me and Maj, for example."

"Well . . ."

"Come *on* . . . !"

Roddy paused, then said angrily, "I don't want to admit anything! Admitting stuff got me *into* this!"

Maj thought privately that Roddy needed some coaching in

cause and effect, but she said nothing for the moment.

"Roddy," Mark said, "building a construct to make people sick in the *first* place got you into this. Don't start getting yourself confused. Now look, shut up and listen to me! You did a smart thing. You were protecting your butt . . . in a crooked kind of way. You had your system mirror hers. So you've got a template of her nervous system squirreled away here somewhere."

Roddy paused for a long moment . . . then nodded.

"Okay," Charlie said. "Mark's right. She comes in here . . . she looks over your shoulder and she co-opts your baby . . . and you mirror her all the time. It's a good thing . . . because it'll save your life."

"It can't," Roddy said. "It's too late for me, don't you understand? She's got the vector already! I gave it to her!"

"The bug itself?" Charlie demanded. "Or just the instructions for how to tailor it?"

"Just the instructions—an edible vector, gastro-resistant. It was the fastest way and she was really pissed off, she wanted it fast, and she said her people would take less time to—"

"Thank God," Charlie said. "Then we still have a chance. Does she want to see you again?"

"Tomorrow. For lunch at Obelisco. For *lunch*!" Roddy was almost in tears, and resisting them mightily. "She'll kill me with the bug I gave her! But I'll have to go! If I don't she'll have me hunted down and they'll throw me in jail!"

"*No* one's going to throw you in jail. She's not Net Force people, whoever she is."

"Then whoever she works for will just hunt me down and kill me!"

"That does seem more likely," Mark admitted. "If I'd given them what you'd given them, *I'd* kill me too. The fewer people know where this came from, the better."

Roddy looked panic-stricken, and utterly wretched. Maj felt for him. At the same time . . . she found herself getting a horrible idea, a *wonderful,* horrible idea . . . and she turned to Charlie, her mouth open to start telling him about it, and saw that she didn't have to. The same idea was already alight in his eyes.

"Yeah," Charlie said. "Oooh, remind me never to get *you* ad at me."

"It's mutual," Maj said, thinking of the Muffin, and of what ight have happened to her, which these people would not ave cared about in the slightest, should there have been some nd of accident and the "internal" version of the plague rned out to be contagious after all. "Roddy, you have to go ave lunch with her."

"She'll kill me!"

"She'll try . . . and you know how. But we can have a little irprise waiting for her. Look—you're not alone on this one. ere's what you do."

The explanations took surprisingly little time. Maj was ither shocked to see how quickly the *gotcha* expression came ack to Roddy's face . . . but this time she thought he might ave had reason.

"Can you do it?" Mark said. "Are you sure? Because if ou can't, the whole thing falls to pieces. We're going to be epending on you."

Roddy stared at him, as if hearing a phrase for the first time. I can do it," he said rather hoarsely.

"Okay. Then get yourself out of here. Enjoy that lunch. I ear Michelin has been getting ready to give the place its first osette. And afterwards, call the number I gave you right way."

Roddy nodded, looking like someone who'd been through oo much in too short a time. He started to walk away into e darkness . . . then paused.

"Why are you doing this for me when I did what I did to ou?" he said, almost inaudibly.

The question that won't go away, Maj thought. *Has the imple tradition of doing good back even when someone tries screw you over gone away so completely from the world?* ut maybe it had. All the better reason to bring it back, then: "golden oldie," as her brother would call it. She had had go look that one up when Rick last used it.

Mark and Charlie stood mute for the moment. "Just go on," 1aj said finally. "Roddy . . . after all this sorts itself out, I ant to talk to you about simming. A lot. But I really don't uch want to talk to you right now at *all,* so I would consider

it a courtesy if you would just go the frack away. We'll s
you tomorrow. You know when.''

Roddy gave her a look that Maj couldn't fathom in th
slightest. Then he was gone.

The shapes in the shadows hurried away, dissolving in th
darkness.

Mark looked after Roddy for a moment. "Really mixed-
guy," he said. "But there's something there to save, I thin
I hope."

"Yeah, well," Maj said. "And what about *us*? Winters
going to be really flamed that we didn't tell him right awa
when all this started to heat up—even though there wasn't
snowball's chance in the Sahara he'd have believed us, it wa
so far out there. I almost wish we had brought him in—w
may need some saving ourselves."

"Oh, come on, we didn't have time," said Mark. "Whe
the pot boils over, what do you do? Run to tell somebody it
boiling? Or take it off the stove yourself?" He shrugge
looked at the complicated programming construct that he wa
almost finished building, and sighed. "Meanwhile, we don
need *this* after all. At least not for its original purpose. How
ever, regarding this Rachel person . . .''

"Yeah," Charlie said. "And those genetically altered *co*
bugs. They're still out there . . . and when they get in here,
they're not dealt with right away, there's going to be trouble.

"So," Mark said, ambling over to look at the structur
Charlie had been building, "are they going to be dealt with?

"Oh, conclusively," Charlie said with a rather feral gri
"I'm gonna see to that. Meanwhile . . ." He looked at the
both. "You two are both about to be pretty sick. Before w
get out of here, you'd better let me give the paramedics a ca
so I can speak medical to them and let 'em know what
expect when they pick you up."

"And what should *we* expect?" Mark said, looking rath
dubious.

"Among other things," Charlie said, "I hope you like
what you had for breakfast, because you're going to see
again. Repeatedly. And many other things you've eaten b
tween childhood and now. Fortunately, there shouldn't be to
many other symptoms . . . which is just as well, because th

nes you do have are going to give you enough to think
bout.''

Maj groaned. ''How long are we going to be sick?''

''Until tomorrow,'' Charlie said. ''The treatment isn't going
o be difficult, and you'll at least be able to go virtual again,
ough they're not going to let you out of bed. But if I were
ou, when the ambulances arrive, get really sick. Look *bad*'' —
nd he grinned—''for the cameras.''

t seemed part of Charlie's nature that just about everything
e said had an air of absolute authenticity, of something that
vas real, or about to be that way. Almost as soon as she went
on-virtual, and frequently over the next twelve hours, Maj
ad reason to curse that fact again and again, for it all came
bout exactly as he had predicted.

She spent those twelve hours throwing up almost nonstop.
Maj did not have to try to look bad for any cameras. It came
nore than naturally for her. As the paramedics were carrying
er out of her house to the medevac unit, she put in her bid
o qualify for the preliminary rounds of the Eastern Division
Projectile Vomiting Finals. In the hospital she had hoped she
vould at least get some sympathy, but by and large the nurses
reated her with a casual and unconcerned compassion, which
uggested that they had seen much better throwing up in their
ime, and that the sooner she got out of their way and left the
ed for someone who *really* needed it, the better they would
ike it. The only consolation, Maj thought, was that the son of
he director of Net Force was almost certainly getting the same
reatment, if not worse.

But it all seemed bad enough at her end. Almost as soon as
he could spend more than five minutes without needing the
ucket, her mother was sitting by her bedside, saying, ''I
alked to James Winters this morning, dear. Maj, I can't be-
ieve you got involved in this without *telling* me!''

She could do little at that point but moan. ''Mom,'' she
aid, ''it all happened so fast. It was kind of like when a pot
oils over on the stove. Do you run off to tell someone it's
oiling, or do you turn it off yourself?''

Her mother sighed, looking surprisingly resigned for some
eason Maj couldn't work out. ''Never mind, honey,'' she

said. "Your father said something similar, God knows why. . . would think you're an experiment in male parthenogenesis, I didn't know better." She started going through the larg beat-up canvas shopping bag that she used as a purse on "no mal" days, if there were any such things around the household. "Ricky says hello, and he wants to know why he started to meet people who say they didn't know he was in simming."

"Oh, jeez," Maj said, having forgotten completely abou masquerading as her brother in Roddy's sim. "Uh, I'll explai it to him later."

"Please do. And the Muffin sent you this." Her mothe extracted a slightly crumpled drawing of something winge which after a little study Maj was able to make out as a *Archaeopteryx*. Writ large at the top of it, slightly shakil were the words I LOV YOU MADY, and under these, I TOLD Y I SA IT.

Maj smiled. "Is she okay?"

"She's jealous. She wants to go for a ride in the noisy flye too, she says."

There was a knock on the door frame, and James Winter stuck his head around it. "Busy?"

"I'm not throwing up at the moment," Maj said, "if it the same thing."

"You'll keep her company, Mr. Winters, will you?" sai Maj's mother. "I have to go off to a PTA thing, and they'r all going to think I'm caught in traffic somewhere." Maj' mother bent over her and smooched her on the forehead. "I' see you afterwards, honey."

Her mom headed out. Winters sat down in the vacated cha and looked around him. "All the requisites of a comfortabl stay, I see."

"The bucket," Maj said, "the inspiring view of the parkin lot, the virt-hookup, which for some reason won't activat Yes, it's all here."

"I wanted a chance to talk to you first," Winters said. "An also, you should take a few hours, at least, to recoup you strength before you dive straight back into virtuality." He sa back, folding his arms and looking around him.

"How's Mark?" Maj said.

"About the same as you."

"Ick," Maj said with feeling.

"Oh, he won't be that way for long," said Winters. "Mark
s a resilient type. And he's feeling pleased with himself,
vhich is Mark's normal state of mind."

Maj smiled very slightly.

"And you?" Winters said. "Are you feeling pleased with
ourself?"

"Should I be?" Maj said.

"Sneaky," said Winters. "If you're trying to finagle me
nto giving you a positive evaluation, I might have to agree
hat one might be forthcoming, with some extenuating circum-
tances."

Maj kept her mouth shut and tried to work out whether this
vas a compliment.

Winters gave her a wry look after a moment. "You found
 nasty situation and you investigated it as covertly as you
 ould," he said. "When it started to blow up in your face,
 ou thought the situation through and acted decisively. And
 vhen it got dangerous, you took the danger where the genu-
 nely committed take it," Winters said. "On yourselves: in
 our own bodies. That kind of commitment requires that it be
 onored at the moment, regardless of what the future may
 old."

"Uh." Maj was not sure about the phrasing on that last
 art. "But how did you—I mean—"

"Mark Gridley," said Winters, "being his father's son and
 herefore a cautious young cuss as regards documentation, rou-
 inely records everything he does—all his virtual experience—
 ack to his own workspace. God only knows what his data
 torage costs per month. So we've seen everything *you* did
 nd said in Roddy's workspace, and by and large I think you
 hree acted responsibly . . . minus a couple of lapses which I
 vill discuss with you and Mark and Charlie at some time when
 wo out of the three of you are able to concentrate profitably
 n something besides the bottom of an emesis basin."

He looked rather severe. Maj gulped, trying hard not to
 hink about the emesis basin, and wondered what she had said
 or done that would be construed as "lapses."

"Meanwhile," Winters continued, glancing out the window

at an ambulance coming in for a landing, "we'll be analyzing
your analysis of the 'mirroring' structure for some time to see
how closely it matches our own, as ours unfolds. But what a
sweet piece of business this is all going to turn out to be, after
the dust settles. L'Officier has genuinely come up with something major here."

"You're not going to throw him in jail or anything, are
you?" Maj said.

Winters regarded her speculatively. "Your father told me
you were going to say something like that," he said. "He says
you describe this behavior as 'not being able to stay mad at
anybody.' A shame we can't find a way to spread *that* virtually
as easily as this bug could have been spread."

"Where do you know Dad from?" Maj said.

Winters got an amused look. "Probably you should ask him
about that. He may tell you. But if he doesn't, you should just
assume that some old connections may be better left unadver-
tised."

Maj blinked at that. Her *father* . . . something weird and secret? The unreconstructed ivory-tower academic? "Wait a
minute, what do you—"

"Meanwhile," Winters said, apparently not noticing the interruption, "as regards Roddy, some of his treatment will depend on how fully he cooperates with us, naturally. But I don't
see any great problems. For one thing, he is being *very* co-
operative. Apparently you three explained matters to him in
terms he understood exactly."

Maj began to wonder which had been more perfect:
Roddy's understanding of the situation's ethics, or of Mark
Gridley and the art of "pulping."

"And for another thing," Winter said, "it would be nuts to
either alienate him, or leave him in a situation where some
other opportunistic group can get their hands on him and force
him to do something similar. The news is out now that a technique of virtual infection may exist. That we're going to do
everything we can to make it look like a *false* rumor won't
help. The genie's out of the bottle, and rumors like this tend
to start people thinking." Winters sighed. "It's better to keep
Roddy under our eye, where we can protect him and his
mother . . . and at the same time help him see what other little

wonders he might come up with, given a free rein and the occasional suggestion. There's no denying that he's already made a tremendous contribution to science, even if he did it under questionable circumstances.''

''What are you going to do about Rachel?'' Maj said.

Winters smiled at that, and the expression was genuinely wintry. ''It's more like what have you *already* done about her, isn't it?''

''Uh, well . . .''

''Seems like a waste of energy to deconstruct an intervention that's in place already and so far along,'' Winters said. ''And so elegantly nasty. Jeez, you and Charlie should be kept far away from each other in future. Like sodium and water. But I think what's going to be done is what you had planned.''

Maj grinned.

''That's exactly what I meant,'' Winters said, shaking his head in resignation. ''I wouldn't miss this for the world . . . and I wouldn't ask you to either. It would hardly be fair to keep you out of the kill. When 'Rachel' goes in . . . we'll flash you the word. There's no reason you can't be there virtually, after all.''

Maj's heart leapt.

''She'll go in, all right,'' Winters said. ''The people who were covertly watching your house and the Gridley place got all the evidence *anyone* could have needed . . . and the people here who've been approached for information have been telling them the most horrible stories. The raging fevers, the convulsions, the whole *buckets* of—''

Maj's eyes abruptly went wide. She pitched hastily over toward the other side of the bed.

''Sorry,'' Winters said, ''I'll call you later, when you're not otherwise occupied, and we'll discuss your further career options. . . .''

Upside down, her head pounding, through the tears and the terrible taste, Maj found that it was still possible to smile, no matter how raw the back of your throat was.

Rachel got to lunch at Obelisco a little early. She greeted the maitre d' with a twenty-dollar handshake, and expressed a desire for a table off to the side, in a quiet spot, as well as a couple of other requests. The table was immediately produced for her, and she sat down and let the waiter bring her a glass of a Grisons-bred *blauer Burgunder* wine, while she admired the sunny decor, the cheerful yellow napery, and golden sponge-stenciled walls, all decorated with coiling hop vines and flowers and wreaths of Graubuendner chiles. The wood-burning grill was full of vine-cutting coals. The steak was supposed to be excellent here, and she intended to find out, since this was on the expense account.

Right on time came Roddy, looking nervous, but also cheerful at the smell that hit him as he came in the door. This was hardly unexpected. Rachel had discovered at their one other lunch that Roddy was a trencherman, one of those people who had had the clean-your-plate, don't-you-know-children-are-starving-on-the-moon ethos beaten into them well past removing. That suited her purposes entirely.

Roddy sat down, and they chatted cheerful nothings over the menu, made their choices, and talked more nothings until the appetizers arrived. Roddy was eager to pump her for information about what was going on, but Rachel had no intention of spoiling his appetite until it had done its job, so she refused charmingly to be drawn in, all through the appetizers of *buendnerfleisch* and *capuns*.

Roddy, having had four glasses of soda water, as a function of his nervousness, now got up and headed off for the men's room. This was something Rachel had seen before. Immediately after that, as Rachel had set it up with the maitre d', the entrees arrived: for her, grilled tournedos of beef with polenta and aubergine salsa; for Roddy, shredded veal *"geschnetzel-tes"* in a cream sauce with morels, and Bernese fried-onion *rösti*. *Perfect,* Rachel thought, and having checked again to make sure Roddy was still out of sight, came out with the little thumb-sized bottle of detector liquid.

It was another of life's little ironies. One of the edible-drug companies, the same one that had made itself famous in the previous century for its shake-on "cures" for flatulence and lactose intolerance, had brought out a shake-on liquid that, when coming in contact with food, immediately fluoresced an unmistakable air-rescue orange if the surface of the food contained any of the "fatal" strains of *E. coli.* Everybody used such "shakies" at the table, as commonly as they might use a small personal bottle of chili sauce or a low-sodium shake-on. Now Rachel carefully shook a little of the "detector" on the food on Roddy's plate (and, palming it, into his drink), peered at the plate for a moment, saw no sign of change, and leaned back again, unconcerned. No one around her would have the slightest interest. No one around her would imagine that the shake-on itself contained *E. coli* of a very specialized kind.

Roddy came back and sat down again, and immediately dug into his lunch as if he had never seen one before and might not again. Well, he wouldn't, not like this, Rachel thought. For some few minutes, conversation flagged while he and Rachel both did justice to their meals. Then, all of the *geschnetz-eltes* and most of the *rösti* gone, Roddy took a long swig of his soda water and said, with the air of someone who wouldn't be put off any longer, "Well . . . now that, you know, the *business* is over with . . . what do we do now?"

"Now," Rachel said. "Well." She temporized, watching him eat, wanting to make sure that enough of the object of this whole exercise was safely down him. "One of the reasons

I wanted to have lunch with you was to finalize our business.''

"Finalize?"

"Mmm, yes, that does sound a little dry. Sorry, the bureaucracy does get to me sometimes. I'm afraid I have to tell you that we won't be needing your services anymore.''

Roddy stopped with his fork halfway to his mouth, gaping at her. "But I thought you said—!"

"Well, I'm sorry. I spoke up for you with Gridley—you know I told you I was going to. But unfortunately, I wasn't able to bend him very far. He really feels that you would be a tainted asset. That business with your friend was bad . . . but when he found out that you had been preparing attacks on a couple of other acquaintances as well . . . I wasn't able to do much of anything to change his mind. Unfortunately, loyalty is considered an important value at Net Force, and when you were able to repeatedly do things like *that* . . . well . . . it did cause a lot of questions to be asked. I'm sorry to have raised any false hopes.''

"And you're just going to take my simming technology, my mirroring, and steal it from me!"

"We can't very well steal what was a gift in the first place,'' Rachel said coolly. "Well, rest assured, this technique will be used in the national interest.'' *Some nation,* she thought with amusement, effortlessly keeping her face straight. *And somebody's interest . . .*

"You can't—I'll, I'll—"

"What? Sue?" She permitted herself just a slim smile. "You can't sue a government agency. Besides, who are you going to tell who'll believe you? And bear in mind the security ramifications that we discussed. Try to raise this matter publicly, and Net Force will deny everything. Not to mention . . . I'll be blunt, Roddy. At the moment, things have worked out well enough that Gridley's willing enough to drop the charges and let you off. Let's call it a little misunderstanding between you and your friends. Something good's come of it, so Net Force won't say anything further. But if you start making noises about this in public . . . then I'm afraid we might have to tell our side of the story in public as well . . . and that would land you straight in a Federal penitentiary. That 'uncomfortable scenario.' ''

He sat there looking stricken, then got up suddenly and lurched off in the direction of the toilets.

Rachel didn't smile, though she felt like it.

Within a couple of minutes Roddy was back. He sat down, drank his drink at a single gulp, and finished his lunch. He seemed to have little more to say to her. She tried to draw him out a little, but she supposed she could understand how annoyed he must be . . . little Mr. Know-It-All suddenly gotten the better of, and so conclusively too.

Rachel sighed and got up to go off to the ladies' room herself, then returned to finish her coffee and deal with the bill. It came. She finished her coffee, corrected a math mistake on the bill, smiled at the annoyed waiter, having gotten the better of him too, and stood. "I have appointments this afternoon," she said softly. "I'm sorry it couldn't have ended more happily for everyone involved. Good-bye, Roddy. Keep your nose clean from now on. There are people watching. . . ."

Rachel got up and made her way toward the entrance. The last thing she saw on her way out, as she glanced back one last time, was Roddy, as he dropped his head onto his folded arms on the table in front of him, his shoulders shaking uncontrollably.

Poor kid, Rachel thought with no particular compunction, and went off to take care of the afternoon's business.

She came into Roddy's workspace quietly, and walked down along the side of the huge construct-cube with confidence—quickly, but not hurrying: someone who had the right to be where she was, and didn't see a need to make anything but prudent haste. She was carrying a cage, rather like a large cat-carrier.

"Visualization scenario two," she said.

She was standing in a box-tree maze: perfectly clipped hedges, standing up square and tall, themselves defining a huge square. She made her way unerringly into the maze, like someone who knows every twist and turn of it, having carefully studied it for a good while.

She came to the center of the maze, and put the cage down. The very center was a perfect square space with a little chicken-wire-covered iron-railing gate across it. Rachel opened the gate, set the cage inside, closed the gate, reached over the gate, and pulled the pin that let the contents of the cage go free.

They tumbled out with a slow, oozing movement. There were six of them. They glistened in the morning sunlight above the maze, their thick skins rainbowy in the clear radiance. Behind them, thin silvery corkscrew tails lashed and pushed them along. They bumped up against the walls of the maze, rebounded, bumped against the gate, rebounded from that.

Rachel stood watching them for a good little while, making sure they couldn't get out before they were wanted. That would be soon enough. She would make her escape, at the same time giving the command that her programmer colleagues had told her would allow the infection out, setting off the time bomb that was ticking inside Roddy even now. As soon as he came into his virtual space again, the infection would take hold. Very shortly he would start feeling unwell. The techs had suggested to her that it should take only a few hours for the major neuropsychiatric symptoms to set in, and the gastrointestinal ones only a little while more. Roddy would be raving within an hour or so, unconscious within a couple of hours more, dead within thirty-six hours . . . forty-eight at the max. It was a shame to lose such a resource . . . but you couldn't make an omelet without breaking the occasional egg. And after this little business, there would be a lot more to keep her busy as the technology was marketed. All subsequent omelets would be stuffed with Beluga caviar, and eaten under a tropical sun by a very well-to-do retiree. . . .

"Ugly-looking bunch of little suckers, aren't they," said a voice, a young voice, one she didn't know. She looked up.

There was not just one person looking at her from across the next-to-last wall of the maze, but three. A small, slender dark-haired youth with some Oriental blood; a brown-haired, brown-eyed girl, older, fair, a little muscular; a black kid, maybe about the same age as the girl, fairly slim. They looked at her with expressions varying from amusement to disgust.

Rachel took a breath. She had no idea who they were: friends of Roddy's maybe. She didn't care. She was armed, and she very much doubted they could do anything to stop her. She opened her mouth. . . .

"Kill visualization," she said.

"Countermand," Mark said.

The maze stayed where it was. Rachel broke out into a sweat, made a move as if to come at them—

"No," Mark said, "you stay right where you are."

She laughed out loud. "Why shouldn't I go exactly where I please? They're not going to—"

. . . and one of the *coli* jumped at her leg.

Rachel backpedaled hurriedly.

"There's a possible reason why you shouldn't," Charlie said. "See, you left a complete immunological and neural record when you came in here last, and, well, we thought that since you'd taken such an *interest* in these bugs—"

"Don't be stupid, kid," Rachel snapped. "They can't do anything to me—"

"Tell *them* that," Maj said. The *coli* kept humping toward Rachel.

"Oh, yeah, well, *you* think you haven't had the live vector," Charlie said. "Unfortunately, you have. And when you went to the bathroom and left Roddy alone at the table, he made sure that your meal was inoculated with the stuff too."

Rachel turned that beautiful face on Mark, her eyes narrowed. "The little bastard son of a bitch," she hissed, "*he set me up!* I'll—"

She started to reach inside her jacket.

One of the *E. coli* jumped at her leg and wrapped itself around it.

Rachel screamed, stood on one foot, and tried scraping it off with the other stiletto heel.

"I doubt that's gonna help much now," Mark said mildly. "See, that's a full-blown infection right there, if I'm not mistaken. Any virtual contact between them and you will do, now that the timer's been set off in your system. What's the timing, Charlie?"

"An hour to early NP symptoms," Charlie said. "Severe headache, severe pain of the spine and joints, increasing intracranial pressure, inflammation of the meninges, and later of the pia mater and the dura mater. Endocrine and paracrine symptoms maybe an hour later: delirium, irrationality, various cortical stuff, maybe even thyroid storm if things get kinky. Hydrocephalus. Eventual congestive heart failure and myelin stripping. Death. Fallen arches, scabies, Waring-blender syndrome—''

Mark looked at him in disbelief. "You couldn't have given her *that*."

"If she had artificial heart valves, and I'd had enough time, I sure could have. And I would have too," he said, and gave Rachel a look so amused and speculative that Maj shivered.

"The death part, though," Mark said, "*that's* for real. Thirty-six hours, 'Rachel.' ''

She was standing very still and pale now. The *coli* had slipped down her leg, unnoticed, and had humped away, looking for somewhere more interesting to be. But Rachel no longer had that choice. She was stuck in VR now. The moment she exited this scenario, her illness would become all too real.

Another form came walking out of the darkness. "I would say," he said, "that you've badly antagonized some of our younger operatives. This tends to be a dangerous business . . . since they're not yet bound by, shall we say, the restraint which they'll eventually learn during their careers." The sidelong look he threw at Mark suggested to Maj that they had had this particular discussion more than once, and probably to no avail.

James Winters came to stand in the middle of the space, and from all around, more shadowy shapes became evident here and there, but they were Net Force operatives, not Roddy's orcs. Winters reached into his jacket pocket and came out with his ID. "Net Force," he said. "And this ID is real. You're under arrest for felony assault, several violations of the chemical and biological weapons codes, and impersonating a Net Force officer."

With a gesture of her hand, Rachel burst out of the maze and fled into the darkness. They went after her. Mark went with them. Winters went after the other operatives, slowly, following the soft alerting calls of people encircling a suspect preparatory to catching her.

"Good," Charlie said. "Come on. One more piece of work

to finish." He nodded off toward where the "maze" had been.
Maj, bemused, went with him.

"Computer," he said, "bring up the wall."

It flashed into being in front of them, burning a soft blue.
It mimicked the turns and angles of the maze that Rachel had
made. "That's the chemical I was building yesterday," Charlie said. "It's an antagonist to the outer shells of *coli*, their
'capsules' . . . there are proteins in it that *coli* doesn't like.
There's a boundary barrier of it right around the edges of
Roddy's workspace, and this inner barrier as well . . . though
it wasn't in this shape originally. Her maze messed it up.
Never mind. Now we go hunting."

"Hunting for what?"

"Those *coli*," Charlie said, heading into the maze. "The
outer 'bugs' won't work without them. These need to be found
and killed right away—we don't dare take the chance that they
might get out of here somehow. Not that it seems likely . . .
but in this case, certainty matters."

"You thought of all this beforehand?"

"It's just simming without the sim" Charlie said softly as
they turned a corner in the maze. "You try to run down all
the options in your head beforehand. That's what doctors do.
Eliminate the impossible . . . treat what's left."

Maj nodded, not wanting to speak at the moment. Her
mouth was going dry again, so that her suggestion that the
full Net Force ops should be allowed to handle this never quite
got out. Besides, there was a look in Charlie's eyes that suggested any such suggestion would have been in vain. *He wants
to get up close and personal with some germs. . . .*

They turned right, then left, then left again.

"You know where we're going?" she said.

"Nope. It was just a nice little corral before."

"Oh, great!" Maj said—and then stopped herself.

A soft sound: something sliding. Like a newspaper on a
slate floor. *Sssshh, sssssh.*

Ssssshh.

"Hear that?" She asked.

Charlie listened. "Yup. That way."

They followed the sound. It didn't move much, or did so
only slowly, so that though they went down a lot of blind

alleys and paths that had nothing but air at the end of them, they still felt they were working closer and closer to the sound. And then they turned a corner—

Maj stopped, her throat seizing up so tight she couldn't get a word out.

In a dead end ahead of them, about ten by ten feet wide, were the *coli*. They were sliding about over one another and the floor, pushed along by the gleaming coiling whips of their flagella. They headed toward the wall sometimes, but bumped it and backed away, grouped together again, and then headed in another direction—the wall again—bumped it, backed away, started off in yet another direction—toward Maj and Charlie, this time—and slowly kept coming, there being nothing to stop them.

"They're, they're not the *real* bacteria," Maj managed to say, and then shook her head at her own obtuseness.

"These guys? Nope. Made about a thousand times bigger for visibility, that's all. They're just the mirrors of the real vector."

"They're too damn real for me," Maj said, watching them come, their tails lashing viciously, each one symbolic of a whole body's worth of infection. She half expected them to snarl. "How are we supposed to handle them?" Maj said. "Whips and chairs?"

"Looks like they've got the whips already," Charlie said. "Think a chair would help?"

"At the moment, *anything* would feel better than standing here empty-handed!"

Charlie reached sideways into the air and handed her a chair. "Here. Keep the rest of them backed into the corner . . . but let one out. I'm going to take a knife to it."

Maj shrugged. The chair was more than symbolic: The "legs" of it were studded with constructs that she guessed were antagonist enzymes keyed to the bug in question. She jabbed at them with the chair.

One of them feinted at the chair, then jumped past her. "Opportunistic little bugs," Charlie said, and suddenly there was an odd knife in his hand, forward-curved and looking deadly sharp on the inside edge.

"Nice," Maj said, glancing at it.

"*Kukri*," Charlie said. "My dad has one." He kept his eyes a the *E. coli* that was slithering toward him, driving itself ong by the flagellum like a crazed watch using its uncoiling atchspring to push itself by.

"That's half the problem," Charlie said. "Little suckers are o mobile by half. Hah—"

He moved so fast that Maj didn't see him launch himself the *coli* as it tried to slip past him. The knife flashed. The agellum flew off to one side, sliced off close to the root. The acterium flopped down on the floor again, tried to hump and ump along as it had before, but couldn't, the stump of the agellum thumping on the floor.

The *coli* hissed. All the others hissed too then, an awful ound that made the hair stand right up on Maj's neck. All of lem jumped at the chair together, and Maj poked and jabbed lem back into place, all of them still hissing. "How are they oing that, it's not like they've got lungs—!"

"It's chemical. You're hearing a chemical trauma mes-lge," Charlie said, kicking the *coli* from which he had am-utated the flagellum. "And for all I know, they can feel each ther's pain or something, they're all almost the same organ-m, nearly clones."

"I thought bacteria had sex," Maj said. "Some of them."

"Some of them do," Charlie said, lifting the knife again, icking a spot. "You wouldn't like what they'd get to be terwards. But *this* one's never going to get the chance to produce."

He drove the knife in deep. There was another hiss, more esperate, and all the others jumped at Maj again.

One of them jumped past her as she poked at them with the air. She flushed, furious, and leapt.

"Watch out for the flagellum, watch out!" Charlie was yell-lg, but Maj was watching for it already. She came down with oth feet on the would-be escapee and squashed it flat.

More hissing, louder, but the others seemed a little less will-lg to jump at her now. Maj jumped off the *coli*—and it tried unsquash itself, its flagellum lashing furiously against the oor.

"They're tough," Charlie said. "It's the encapsulation.

Here.'' He bent over it with the knife, slashed. Cytoplas
spilled out. He was careful not to touch it.

"What about the flagellum?" Maj said, turning her attentic
back to the four *coli* left in the corner. "Is there toxin on
or something?"

"Don't know," Charlie said. "Didn't want you to find ot
the hard way, though."

She had no desire to. "Come on," she said, feeling faintl
sick—not really a challenge after the last twelve hours or s
"Let's finish them off."

They did, one at a time. It took a while before Charlie wa
gazing down at the last one, its flagellum already sliced of
He said softly, "Wish I could do the same to all your bud
dies," and drove the knife in deep.

The last hiss of pain slowly died away. "Wall subroutine,
Charlie said. "Any more of these?"

"No. All confirmed dead."

"Open inner wall."

It vanished. Out in the main workspace, a small knot of No
Force people was coming more or less toward them, holdin
someone between them. Mark was walking ahead of the grou;
"Hey, where were you?" he said.

"Unfinished business," Charlie said, and cheerfully thre
the *kukri* up in the air. It vanished. "A little disinfection."

They stood together as the group of Net Force operative
caught up with them. They had Rachel, with her hands re
strained behind her, and a look of unrestrained fury on he
face. Behind the group came James Winters.

"Ms. 'Halloran' here has agreed to tell us everything w
want to know about the people she's working with," Winte
said, "and as a result, they will all shortly be joining her in
place suited to quiet reflection. In exchange, we'll have o
techs defuse her infection, and we'll spend a good while e
amining this structure to see what else it can do for the huma
race." He nodded casually to the three Explorers. "Thanks
you."

Rachel threw a deadly look at the three of them. "I ho
we meet again," she said, "under more propitious circur
stances."

The Net Force people took her away. Winters looked aft

em, then said, "Two of you better get back to the hospital. harlie, we'll be wanting to see you later in the week about is, and you, Mark. We need some annotation on your ad- tions to the main sim. Oh, and Maj . . ."

He tossed her a chip. Surprised, she caught it.

"From a friend. Run it in your workspace when you get me." Winters looked up at the construct. "Nice work," he id, and turned away.

The three looked at each other, and followed him into the rkness.

was another day before Maj could run the chip. The doctors the hospital were antsy about letting her out quickly, con- lering the cause of her illness, but finally everyone was reed that there was no reason to keep her any longer. Her d came to take her home, and she thought about asking him question . . . then restrained herself.

The kitchen was blessedly empty and quiet when she got , her brother and the Muffin and her mother all off some- here else. Maj sat down at the kitchen table in the implant air and brought up her virtual workspace, half and half with e kitchen.

The chip was on the kitchen table, along with her knapsack d much other stuff. "Play that," she said to her computer, eling suddenly almost too tired to be curious.

A pause.

Darkness—

—over the tarmac at Muroc. The sky was indigo, blazing th stars: Frost feathered the weeds at the edge of the con- ete in front of the hangar. Off past the runway, out among e Joshua trees and tumbleweed, a mockingbird was singing rious descants at the unheeding stars. Maj rose slowly from r chair, looking toward the long dark shadow sitting there, hile out in the darkness the mockingbird started doing a bad itation of someone starting up a jet engine. . . .

Maj took a long breath of the cold, cold air. "Describe e," she said. "Is there any message with it?"

"Sim program file, written with DelEx authoring tool, ver- on 4.0," said the computer. "File title MADDY2.DLXAT. xt message accompanying."

The original file. My original file. Uncorrupted! ''Displa
the message,'' Maj said.

Huge letters of fire appeared against the night, illuminati
the silvery shape of the Valkyrie behind them.

ALWAYS KEEP A BACKUP, they said, and from som
where out by the mockingbird came the sound of Roddy
laughter.

Maj paused for a long moment . . . and then laughed to
and very softly said what he would certainly have said:

''Gotcha.''